WAS THE EVIL IN EILEEN HERSELF?

Or was she, as they said in the village, a witch like her great-grandmother Monica?

Eileen was afraid. Very afraid. But she had to stay now. She had to find out if she was truly one of the damned...

Also by Claudette Nicole
The Mistress of Orion Hall
Bloodroots Manor
Circle of Secrets
The Dark Mill
The House at Hawk's End

THE HAUNTING OF DRUMROE

CLAUDETTE NICOLE

Copyright © 1971 by Jon Messmann

The characters and events portrayed in this book are fictitious. Any similarity to real persons, living or dead, is coincidental and not intended by the author. No part of this book may be reproduced, or stored in a retrieval system, or transmitted in any form or by any means, electronic, mechanical, photocopying, recording, or otherwise, without express written permission of the publisher.

ISBN-13: 978-1-957868-23-3

Published by
Cutting Edge Books
PO Box 8212
Calabasas, CA 91372
www.cuttingedgebooks.com

CHAPTER ONE

THE NIGHT was a giant bird of blackness that wrapped its wings around the earth, settling down over each hamlet and village, each field and meadow, each lake and mountain. It turned the sweet land of Donegal in the upper north corner of Ireland from a warm and winning place into a stark and stygian world. In this world the creatures of night came forth, the wailing, wandering, homeless spirits of the lost, the banshees and the forces of darkness, and the powers of evil set free by the giant bird of night. And, as it settled itself on the land, and the warmth of its great black body touched the ground, a sweeping grayness of mist rose up to further cloak the creatures of the night, an ethereal blanket that turned the real into the unreal and substance into shadow.

On this night, swept by the shrouded mists, there were those who crept through the dark, hunched over like goblins, silent as serpents. They were treading—not on the dew-wet forest fern but on the edge of an abyss, the pit of the damned—and so they hid from the day. There were others who reveled in the mist-laden blackness, hiding—not from the day but from the tortures of their own souls. And there was one more who came on feet as soft as the gray mist, a messenger of death, eager to stain the night with the dark red of blood.

It was little wonder, then, that the wail of the night wind fell against windows tightly shuttered and doors well latched. The good people of County Donegal left the night to lovers, fools, and those who had to be about in it; it had always been so in this land of contrasts, of softness and hardness, warmth and cold rigidity, faith and superstition, beauty and pain, yesterday's hates and tomorrow's hopes.

Just at dusk the great silver plane had landed at Shannon Airport, and the girl was waiting for the rent-a-car agency to process a car for her. She had hair the color of burnished copper, skin a cream white, and eyes of dark blue. Her face was fine, proud, and altogether beautiful. Like the girl in the poem by William Butler Yeats, she had "... red, mournful lips and seemed the greatness of the world in tears."

"I'm afraid it will take a while, Miss Donegan," the girl from behind the agency desk said. "We have been short-handed today. Why don't you have dinner in the airport lounge while you're waiting?"

Eileen ran a hand through her dark copper hair. It was a good suggestion and she turned to go into the muted pleasantness of the dining lounge. Eating here would save time and she might not find anyplace open on the long drive. This wouldn't be an American turnpike with periodic all-night dining places, she reminded herself. Not that she minded night driving. She preferred it in some ways. But then she'd always had a strange attraction for the night. Her tall, lithe beauty brought stares as she followed the hostess to a small corner table. She was glad she'd decided to wear the soft lavender sweater and the tweed skirt. Eileen sat back, sighed deeply, and ordered a whisky first, then *colcannon*, that wondrous mixture of green cabbage, mashed potatoes, scallions, and roast beef: in this instance, though, any number of meats were used in the dish. Looking out the large window she could see airport workers in jackets. The feeling of anticipation and warmth inside her was both annoying and surprising. It was as though she were a sailor home from the seas, a wanderer returning from far-off lands. It was disconcerting. She had always prided herself on being above excursions into Irish sentimentality. Yet here she was, feeling sentimental as a schoolgirl looking over her scrapbook of mementoes, perfectly aware that her feelings were selfgenerated. After all, she'd left Ireland when she was a little girl of ten and now she was twenty-seven, seventeen years older and seventeen years wiser. She half-laughed to herself. Perhaps not wiser, she corrected, but certainly more scarred.

As she sipped her drink she took the letter from her purse and placed it on the table beside her plate. Only three days ago it had come to her in New York, and now as she stared at the envelope she wondered how she should properly address her aunt when they met, as Aunt Agnes or Lady Donegan, Mistress of the House of Drumroe, the house of the red ridge. Over the years as a girl growing up in America, it had always been "Aunt Agnes" in the letters they had exchanged. But letters from a young girl and a personal meeting are two different things, Eileen knew. She rested her slender hand on the envelope. It had been a strange letter with its note of urgency in almost every sentence. Yet, for her, it had come at precisely the right moment. What strange concordance of events had brought it about, she asked herself. What made things happen when and as they did? The question often occupied her thoughts. Was it all just so much chance, so much meaningless coincidence? She'd never been able to accept that. There had been too many unexplainable things to cast it all aside as mere happenstance. Her thoughts flashed back to that first remembered time, that night when she'd awakened in terror, screaming that someone in the family was dying a violent death. Two days later the wire came telling of her nephew Terence Mulcane. He'd been fished from the Clare River, victim of a boating accident. Not more than a year later she'd grown cold with fear one morning and cried out Cyril Donegan's name. That very day her elderly uncle was killed in a fall from the Belfast-Dublin Express.

She'd been only twenty that first time and it had frightened her terribly, especially when she thought about the family history—an ancestor, Monica Donegan, had been burned as a witch in 1790. But this was the twentieth century and people were avid believers in coincidence or in a rational explanation for everything. And so, when her strange premonitions occurred, she remembered not to be frightened and settled merely for being thoroughly shaken each time. Some years later she had attended a few sessions on extrasensory perception, but quit when she realized they raised more questions than answers.

The waitress brought her *colcannon* and she ate slowly, watching the lights come on across the flat expanse of the airport. She squinted, trying to see beyond them, to pierce the darkness. Out there lay the land she wanted to know once again, another reason she had been so quick to respond to Aunt Agnes's letter. The letter had, in its own way, been a ray of hope unexpectedly flashed into the very dim world in which she found herself.

All the drifting truths had come to a halt by then and hung in the air as grim reminders of her own foolishness and her own mistakes. She had thought, more and more often during the last two years, of returning to her homeland. It hadn't been curiosity or nostalgia that prompted her thoughts. It was simply that if you were starting over it seemed right to start from the beginning, to try to rediscover yourself with old memories, old roots. Sometimes, she had told herself, you had to step backward to go forward.

She forced her eyes away from the dark beyond the dancing lights and finished her meal. When the waitress brought her coffee Eileen opened the letter. Once again she read its carefully composed prose. Aunt Agnes's sentences always said more than the words alone, and this letter was a perfect example of that. Eileen read it softly to herself.

> My Dearest Eileen,
> Recently I had cause to review the affairs of the House of Drumroe, and realized certain facts. For one thing,

other than myself, you are the only living blood descendent of the founder of Drumroe, Lord Kevin Donegan.

Those who would have been in line to take title to the House of Drumroe have all, over these past years, met with one unfortunate tragedy after another. Perhaps, once, we were all guilty of a terrible wrong. I say "perhaps," because to this day I cannot make myself believe that.

In any case, my dear, you stand to inherit the House of Drumroe should something happen to me and I am, alas, an old woman now. There is much I must discuss with you. There are things of today you must know and things of yesterday you should know.

Most immediate, my dear, is the need for your signature on certain deeds and documents. I was going to send them to you, but my solicitor was most adamant you come in person to sign them.

I ask you to come as quickly as possible. A check for your plane fare is enclosed. I look forward to seeing my only niece after all these years.

Love,
Aunt Agnes
Lady Donegan of Drumroe

Eileen recalled how her first reaction had been a kind of disbelieving shock, yet she knew Aunt Agnes would be completely serious about such matters. As a little girl, before coming to the States, she had visited the great House of Drumroe. Its awesome starkness still stayed with her. The thought of herself as mistress of it was beyond belief, but the idea of seeing her aunt again, of going back to the land of her birth, had sent a wave of excitement through her.

Then something else had come to her, the realization that the letter meant a chance to get away, to find a new start for herself. Not as the new Lady of Drumroe, of course. That she'd dismissed at once. Whatever papers needed her signature were a mere formality, an anticipation of possible events. When Aunt Agnes passed on one day, someone would be required to legally negotiate and administer the estate, if for nothing more than to deal with the authorities about the great old manor house. She'd heard that the government was interested in preserving many of the old houses as landmarks. So the practical side of the trip didn't excite her, but going back to find her roots did. It was only after she'd read the letter for the second time that the sense of urgency and alarm in it came through to her, and with each reading that smoldering quality grew stronger. Putting the letter back into its envelope, she paid the waitress and walked from the dining lounge, her long, slender body moving like a willow wand softly blown in the wind.

The car turned out to be a small English Ford. After checking that her bags were all in the rear seat, Eileen slid behind the wheel and drove from the circuitous roads of the airport. Once beyond them she pulled to the shoulder of the road to consult the map that lay atop the dashboard. She decided to take the link roads north to Gort and then go inland some to Ballinasloe. She put the map on the seat beside the letter and her purse. Next to it was the small plastic folder containing the car registration and rental details. *Eileen Donegan,* the sticker on the folder said as she looked down at it. *Eileen Donegan,* the envelope with her aunt's letter in it echoed. It was a nice name. She'd always felt sorry for people who didn't like their names. *Eileen, Eileen,* she said to herself and her full, red lips fashioned themselves into a wry smile. *Eileen!* She repeated the name again, saying it softly. Once she had looked it up in the dictionary and the big, commanding volume had said: *Celtic, of uncertain meaning.* It had its own appropriateness, that, for her life had been a thing of uncertain meaning. As she moved back onto the road, watching the road sign that pointed north, she thought back on that life of uncertain meaning.

The early years were growing years, she and her mother alone, her father dead in a dock accident where he'd worked. She'd taken some of her independence from her mother, who had worked long hours at a department store so they needn't "want for the necessities." Aunt Agnes and other relatives had sent things, of course, but they had learned to do so tactfully, only at those times and occasions when not to accept would have been impolite. Most of her stubbornness was like her burnished copper hair—her very own, and her beauty and stubborn independence had caused many an outer and inner clash. Later, as she went through two years of college before her mother took sick, she learned how easily her beauty brought men to her and how quickly her demands sent them away. She learned how hard it was to be wanted for herself, the person, and not just for her long loveliness, her full ripe breasts, and fire-touched hair.

"Hell," Ed Carter had said to her at a dance one night, "what's wrong with being wanted because of your looks? Be glad for it. It's reason enough."

But it wasn't reason enough, not to her. It wasn't that she didn't like being sought after and admired. She liked being beautiful and didn't deny that, but it wasn't enough. She knew that beauty could betray. She knew she could betray herself with it and, worse, she could betray others as well. That was the thing she dreaded most. And, of course, she had eventually fallen prey to that very dread. Eileen recalled how, when her mother died, she'd taken a new apartment and a new job, plunging into a circle of gay, sophisticated friends, cocktail parties, long weekends, and a terrible searching cloaked in a hundred different disguises. Sometimes the job made the searching even worse. She'd become an interviewer and job analyst for one of the larger employment agencies, and her days were spent with people searching for new jobs, better jobs, a way and a place that would bring them more money, more fun, more contacts, more happiness. It seemed that everyone in the world was searching and she was just one more seeker, looking for a goal she couldn't even clearly define. She recalled how one time, in a particularly low mood, she had written to Aunt Agnes and had received a letter which, typically, said more than she'd been able to comprehend at the time. But, brightened by the light of retrospective clarity, it had stayed in her mind.

"Of course you do not search alone," Aunt Agnes had written. "It is an endless circle. The humble search for wealth, the wealthy search for beauty, the beautiful search for wisdom, and the wise search for humility, and it goes on and on because most often they look in the wrong places."

She knew about looking in the wrong places, Eileen said to herself grimly. She knew all too well.

The girl closed the car window almost to the very top, leaving only an inch of air space. She was into rolling black hills and the night had turned chill. She drove at a comfortable speed on the narrow, winding roads, unlighted and lonely except for the sweep of her headlights which revealed quick glimpses of stone fences, hedges, and open meadows. A small sports car overtook and passed her, but there were very few other cars and none of the huge, thundering, lumbering trucks of American roads. She never thought the time would come when she'd miss their frightening roar and huge bulk. Now she wished for one or two, at least. Not till now did she realize how lonely a road could be without them. She reached out and slipped the letter on the seat into her purse. Her fingers touched the small, cold metal circle inside her purse and she flinched. Damn, she thought angrily. She'd intended throwing the ring away before boarding the plane. For a brief second she thought of stopping and doing so now, but she kept on. It didn't make that much difference, anyway. It was but a symbol, and now just a reminder of things she'd had to put away. She had thrown Chuck away and that was the important thing. Poor Chuck, she didn't even hate him anymore—handsome, charming, witty, empty Chuck. All she hated now was the three-and-a-half lost years in a lost marriage, and the terrible hollowness that comes with a feeling of defeat and doubt.

The divorce had become final only last week and she'd been alone six months then, or almost alone. She wouldn't have thought that final bit of paper would have mattered so. But it had, the terrible finality of it had gotten to her. There'd been so few who had understood, not her circle of gay, new friends, not the other young wives her age, none of those who secretly delight in seeing others suffer for their mistakes. They were stubborn, callous, unfeeling and had called her mixed-up, unfair, and a lot of other things. She still felt the hurt of her wounds. In an ironic way their determined refusal to understand had helped her, for it made her hold fast to her decisions.

There had been a few with kindness, even when they didn't approve or understand. Miss Howell at the agency had held out cool wisdom and friendship during that period of trial. And Father Ryan at St. Joseph's tried in the only way he could, and she was grateful to him for that. His disapproval was honest and his respect for her convictions was equally so. And Sam and Sarah Grossman across the hall from her had shown humanity and goodness. Ever since she'd moved into the building, before Chuck had entered her life, they'd made her into a kind of adopted daughter. They'd understood her days of searching and her days of decision, perhaps because Sam and Sarah had a heritage of searching.

So, three days ago when the letter from Aunt Agnes had come, she'd told the Grossmans about it at once. They were as excited as she was, and she cabled her aunt at once after she'd made plane reservations, telling of her plan to rent a car at Shannon and motor the rest of the way to Drumroe. Estimated arrival time, she had said, midnight Wednesday. The Grossmans had promised to water her plants and take in all the mail until they heard further from her. "I may only be a week or I might stay a month or maybe I'll stay forever," Eileen had said laughingly, though the last part of her sentence had been pure dramatic license. She had no intention of anything more than a visit to sign the papers her aunt wanted signed, to take the time to forget what needed forgetting, and to find old roots and new meanings.

In three days, then, her life had taken a new, twisting turn, a note of hope for a change, and now she shook her head vigorously to clear it of the images of the past. She concentrated on the winding blackness of the road, squinting as she peered ahead, trying to see beyond the headlights' farthest beams. She had no way of knowing of the letter that had arrived at her doorstep less than an hour after she'd taken off from Kennedy Airport. It was marked Air Mail, Special Delivery, and Sarah Grossman had taken it from the postman when she heard him ringing Eileen's doorbell. She had shown it to Sam and they'd both frowned as they read the small, neatly printed return address on the envelope. "Inspector's Office, Scotland Yard, London, England," Sam had read aloud. His wife looked up at him. "Now why would Scotland Yard be writing to Eileen?" she asked. Sam shrugged.

"She promised to be in touch soon," he said. "All we can do is wait till then."

They carefully put it in the corner of the desk in the living room where they had cleared a place to keep Eileen's mail.

CHAPTER TWO

THE GIRL drove through the dark and sleeping towns with names that rolled from the tongue like music. The touch of the land was in those names, the scent of the peat bogs, the feel of the crags and the morning dew, the flavor of a people and the echoes of another time. The signposts ticked off, one after another, as she sped through the night, Athlone, Kiltoon, Ballymahon, Cloondara, Roslea, Donagh. Her neck ached and was stiff and her shoulders hurt but she kept on, the lonesome roads seeming without end. She'd driven through County Galway, Roscommon, skirted the corner of Leitrim, cut through Fermanagh, and into Donegal, and with each mile the night wrapped itself tighter and tighter around the little car. She had driven through long stretches of mist, into steep valleys, over mountain roads, past level pastures and sharp, dangerous cliffs. The fog and mists stayed and then went away and then came again, and the moon played tag with her as she drove on in the lonely, dark land. She was physically tired, but she was on edge. The terrible apprehension had done it, starting soon after she set out toward Donegal. By the time she swung onto the shore road it had seized her in an iron grip, no longer to be denied, no longer to be ignored. At first, she told herself, it was merely a sense of uneasiness at the coming meeting with Lady Donegan. But inside, Eileen knew she lied to herself.

Ever since that night more than seven years ago when she'd wakened screaming, seeing the death of her nephew in a strange and frightening vision, she had come to know the impossibility of denying these strange excitations when they came upon her. Sometimes they were crystal clear, sometimes no more than murk-filled warnings, but always they were terrifying, flooding her with a helpless fear. Eileen Donegan felt, at those times, as though she were controlled by a force from outside, a power beyond her ability to combat. Now, driving through the silent, inky night, that feeling had come to her again, and all her logical, rational reasons failed to satisfy or still the fright inside her. This night there was no clarity, no certain visions, only the apprehension of danger, of trouble, of evil.

Angrily, she pulled off to one side of the road, got out, and stretched her aching arm and shoulder muscles. She walked around the car and tried to let the chill of the night chase away the thoughts that had crept up on her during the long, lonesome, exhausting drive. She heard the sound of a brook racing down an incline and knew that in the warm sun of the day it must indeed be a pretty, beguiling sight. Now it was a wild sound of racing water in the dark, and she got back into the car and drove on again. She was glad she had decided on wearing the sweater and skirt, for the night was cold. Her eyes peered ahead, and finally she saw a small sign marking the dirt road which cut across the land north to the far end of Donegal and the village of Cladvale. The House of Drumroe stood just this side of the village. Eileen swung onto the narrow road and the mist immediately rolled over her in gray-blanket folds. She saw that on the map the road wound along the edge of a U-shaped *lough*, a lake that sent the mists spreading out in all directions from it. The trees lined both sides of the road and bent low to scrape the top of the car, the mist turning their branches into crooked arms and bony fingers. Eileen grew angry with herself as the fear inside her continued to churn and grow. The years had taught her the folly of ignoring the strange certainties that swept over her. She didn't really know which was worse, the terrible things that sometimes came to her or the fear of what strange powers and forces could seize her.

What was it that lay inside her, that rose up unasked, unwanted, an unwelcome visitor that refused to be denied?

Eileen felt the tiny beads of perspiration stand out on her skin, chilling her. She cranked the window up further until there was just a narrow slot of air coming into the car. Only the hum of the engine broke the stillness as she drove, more slowly now in the thick mist, leaning forward over the wheel, peering ahead. She could smell the dampness of the lough and every so often a cloud of mist shredded to let her glimpse the water just off the right side of the road. She kept the headlights on low beam, letting the light pick out the edge of the road. It was exhausting, difficult driving and she felt a wild unexplained fear inside her, a sense of something beyond apprehension now, a sense of impending danger. Her wrist watch, glowing softly green in the dark, told her it was nearly midnight. She ought not to have much further to go. The great House of Drumroe would rise up first, standing between her and the village. The map had shown another road that would have taken her around a big hook and through the village first. The road around the lough was a good ten miles shorter but she hadn't counted on the heavy mist. Yet, anyone such as herself, new to the land, would have taken the lough road. It was, and she smiled as a bit of native tongue leaped out from her dim childhood, the *shan* road, the old road to town. The mind is a funny thing, the girl told herself, filled with bits and pieces and snippets of things we think forgotten but, on the contrary, are really only lying quietly, waiting to be called upon.

Eileen frowned suddenly. Ahead of her a faint red glow colored the gray mist. She continued on and the glow grew stronger. It appeared to be directly ahead on the road. It wasn't strong enough to be an emergency road flare, even in the thick mist. It's glow was soft and steady. A wind, hardly more than a sudden puff, shredded the mist from in front of her, and the road half-cleared for a brief moment. The glow was coming from a lantern, a red lantern placed in the middle of the road, obviously put there as a warning signal. Eileen drove up to halt a few feet from it. She was about to turn off the engine and get out of the car for a better look around when she heard a sharp, sudden crack and then the sound of tearing, splintering bark. She turned to the left and saw the huge dead tree, its leafless branches like so many twisted crutches pointed upward, toppling down onto her. The tree was gathering speed and force as it toppled; in two seconds it would be upon her. Eileen's foot hit the gas pedal in an automatic reaction, and her hands spun the wheel to the right. The little car shot forward and to the right, but the tree smashed down on the back of it. Eileen felt the front end come up off the ground, and the car was flung forward as though a giant hand had slapped it. When the front end hit the ground again, the car was plunging down a short embankment. She felt rather than heard it hit the water, a sudden vibration of shock running through it and instantly the wet blackness closed in around her, a trickle pouring in through the slit of the window at her side. The car was still sinking under the water, but slowly now, as though it were taking part in some languorous underwater ballet. But, Eileen realized in horror, death was the ballet master here.

Later she was to look back in wry amusement at her automatic reactions, but she hooked her purse around her arm, unthinking, just doing things out of habit, and pressed against the door. It refused to give. The car had come to a stop now, half over on its side, and again the girl flung herself against the door with all her strength. It held fast. Eileen felt how quickly, even through the tiny slit that was open, the water was filling the inside of the car. Suddenly, from her days at college, she recalled something about equalization of pressure and taking a deep, deep breath, she rolled down the window. The water poured in over her at once and fighting down the panic inside her, she forced herself to cling there against the dashboard as the inside of the car began to quickly fill. When the car was almost full, she pushed herself against the door. It came open and she was outside, striking for the surface, her lungs burning, ballooning up inside her. She swam frantically and felt her head growing dizzy, light, her strength suddenly slipping away. And then, unable to hold out any longer, she breathed and the water rushed into her mouth. But there was air with it, air that hit her face as she broke the surface, and she gagged, spit out the water, and inhaled deeply. The mists had lifted somewhat and were now wispy vapors trailing along the water. She saw she was close to the dark outline of the bank with a row of trees and bushes just to the right. She treaded water, giving herself time to regain strength and say a prayer of thankfulness, and then she moved slowly to the bank. In the black shadows of the trees that lined a hundred yards or so of the bank, she pulled herself half-out of the water and rested against the inclined side of the soil, hearing the heavy beat of her heart.

There were shore grasses and small bushes, and she pulled herself up on them and rested again on the top of the bank. The bank itself, she saw, was not more than three feet down from the top, and the car had gone off it just where the line of trees came to an end. From where she lay she could see the big, black shape of the tree lying across the road, and she put her head down, shivering, to pull her thoughts together. She was alive, but only by split seconds. The tree would have killed her had it hit the car fully. It surely would have done so, had she shut off the engine. Even so, she'd barely cheated death as the car plunged into the lough.

Eileen frowned suddenly and lifted her head to look out toward the tree as it lay across the road. The red glow of the lantern ought to be clearly visible from where she lay, but there was nothing. Perhaps the tree had smashed it. She got up, fighting down another shiver that ran through her body, and stood for a moment, holding onto a sapling for support. She glanced down at the purse still hooked around her arm and half-smiled. The mist-laden grass was soft and she stepped forward on it out of the line of trees. She moved toward the fallen tree that now lay across the road from side to side. What had made it fall, she questioned herself. No lightning in a storm-swept night had struck it. There had been no great rush of wind to topple it. It had just come down as though an invisible giant hand had pushed it. She stood before it looking down, and her eyes swept over the ground where the red lantern had stood. But it wasn't there. Eileen walked around the tree and went to the other side, but the lantern was not there, either. She searched the ground nearby and got down on one knee to peer along the bottom of the tree. It rested an inch or so from the ground on the shattered stumps of its branches. The lantern wasn't smashed beneath it, either.

Frowning, Eileen got to her feet. She went to the bank and saw the indentations of the car's tires in the soft, moist soil. Then she went back to the road and the fallen tree. Perhaps the lantern had rolled over the bank and into the lough, she conjectured. But even as she held the thought, she flung it aside angrily. The lantern had sat smack in the center of the road. If the tree had come down on it, it would simply have been smashed or knocked aside. And neither of those things had happened. Eileen felt the sudden dryness of her throat, the only part of her that was dry. The lantern was gone. Someone had come and taken it away. She felt the muscles of her jaw twitch as she clambered over the tree and started to walk on up the road, her mind whirling with ugly thoughts.

The entire thing had happened so fast. It had only taken seconds for her to plunge down the bank and into the lake. Even though it had seemed like an eternity when she was trapped under the water inside the car, she knew that it had only been a minute or so. It was possible that a watchman, perhaps asleep on the hill, had heard the crash of the tree, wakened, retrieved the lantern, and left, unaware of the car that had plunged into the lough. It was possible, she said grimly, but damned unlikely. And if so, why hadn't he put the lantern atop the fallen tree to warn others of the obstruction across the road?

The girl shivered and, though she was cold and wet, she knew she shivered for other reasons. Had this been the explanation for the dread that had gripped her as she drove toward Drumroe? A stubborn rebellion was taking its place alongside the cold fright that filled her. She'd had enough of insights and premonitions. She'd thought that here, perhaps, everything would be different. They were a gift, her insights and premonitions, someone had once told her. Well, they were a gift she didn't want and that did her no damn good when she needed it. But, even as she had the thought, she half-retracted it. Perhaps someone else would have shut off the engine and been crushed under the tree. Her sense of impending danger had prevented that. God, there are so many hidden reasons for the things we do, she thought angrily. Even the reasons which seem so clear are so often wrapped in disguises. How painfully well did she know that, she reminded herself.

Suddenly she was conscious of the fact that she was shivering violently and was cold, wet, and thoroughly miserable. The lavender sweater clung to her, outlining the high curve of her breasts almost as though she had nothing on at all. The mists continued to evaporate in a night wind that had sprung up, and she could see the lough on her right as the road curved. To her left more trees, and beyond them, the beginnings of a rise in the land. She found herself walking up a slight incline and around a slow turn when she saw the small, neat sign: DRUMROE. Walking faster, new excitement pulling her on, the road growing steeper. The trees, interlocking branches overhead, turned the path inky black as she picked her way along. She rubbed her arms to keep the circulation in them and then, suddenly, the trees ended and she stood at the edge of a lawn, the towering shape of the house rising up in front of her. Beyond it the dark outline of woods, and beyond the woods the line of a high ridge. As she stared up at the great house the years leaped backward and she was a little girl, looking up at it in almost the exact spot she stood now. It was even more stark and commanding than she remembered it, and she felt its presence reach out to envelop her. Stone at the bottom with wood on the upper floors, gabled roofs and rounded corners reflecting the strange echoes of English tudor and of ancient Celtic *cahir,* or stone fort. It certainly was a part of the surrounding land, and yet it seemed to stand alone, aloof. It had a powerful beauty to it, even in the dark, but it was the beauty of the severe, the unyielding, almost a threatening kind of beauty.

It was wrapped in blackness with not a light on; she frowned. Her cable had been delivered, the cable company had assured her. Yet from the looks of this great house, she wasn't expected at all. A body-wracking shiver shook her long, slender frame, and she hurried forward through the black shadows of the House of Drumroe. She felt terribly small as she stood before the thick, carved oak door. The round door knocker was cold to the touch and made her shiver again. She pounded three times and waited. There was no answer. She pounded again as hard as she could. There was still no sign of life, no light from inside. Her teeth were chattering and she trembled constantly now. Angrily, she pounded again. There had to be some rational explanation for this. When there still was no answer, she started to turn away to try and find an open window or some other way to get out of the cold night wind. There were barns or garages at one side she had noted. Perhaps she could find a way in through them. She had stepped back from the house when she suddenly saw the light come on through the narrow, frosted glass panel alongside the front door. She turned and waited as the door opened slowly. A man stood there, barefoot, with a long coat over pajamas. By the light from the hallway behind him she saw his gaunt face, hollow-eyed as a cadaver, sunken cheeks and burning, deep eyes. Black hair fell across his forehead and, though he was slightly stooped, he seemed as tall as a weathered tree. Like Drumroe, there was a threatening, almost ominous air about him.

"I'm Eileen Donegan," she said. "Lady Donegan is expecting me."

The girl saw the man's deep eyes roam across her face, dropping down to linger on the way her sweater pressed flat against her breasts. His impassive stare shifted back to her eyes.

"Where is Lady Donegan?" Eileen asked, wishing she didn't feel so much like a half-drowned cat. "What happened to my cable?"

"What cable is that, miss?" the man said, his voice the rasp of a steel file.

"My cable," Eileen said exasperatedly. "The cable I sent from New York. I'm her niece."

The man's eyes traveled down her body again and she felt angry at herself for having to explain. "I had an accident," she said, bearing down on the last word. "My car went into the lough. Where is Lady Donegan?"

"She went away suddenly," the man said. "Yesterday."

"Went away?" Eileen frowned. "Where? She was expecting me?"

"I wouldn't know about that, miss. She wasn't here when I got back from town yesterday," he said. "She didn't come back today."

The girl's temper began to rise, pushing aside all fear and cold and confusion. She'd almost been killed in a decidedly strange accident, she was wet and shivering, her aunt wasn't even here to greet her, and this cavernous-faced man kept her standing in the doorway.

"Then I'll just wait for Lady Donegan's return," Eileen said, stepping forward, her head high. "Who are you?"

"Brannock's my name," the man said. "I'm the general handyman here at Drumroe." He stepped back as Eileen pushed past him into a huge, oak-paneled foyer.

"Surely you've a guest room or two in this vast place, Brannock," Eileen said tartly, returning the man's deep, hostile stare. The black fire in Brannock's eyes flickered out and he turned, closing the door after him. He marched past the girl, took a small kerosene lamp from a sideboard, turned it on, and started up a wide flight of carpeted steps. Eileen followed him, pausing to glance into the darkened living room on the right and, opposite it on the left, the stately dining hall. The sight of the long oak table jogged her memory again and she recalled a dinner there once as a little girl. But she didn't pause for memories and hurried after the man as he mounted the stairway. The second-floor hall, deep and wide, was hung with tapestries. Brannock opened the door of a room, lighted a lamp inside, and showed Eileen into the large, heavily draped guest room, a double bed at one wall, tall french windows on an adjoining wall.

"Thank you," she said, holding herself very still, refusing to shiver though she was cold to the bone. "I'll look into things in the morning."

"As you say, miss," the man said, deferential politeness without meaning in his voice. He closed the door and Eileen, glad to see the heavy iron bolt, slipped it into place at once. Tossing off wet clothes as she went, Eileen hurried to the bathroom and turned on the hot water tap. It wasn't the kind of hot water she'd grown accustomed to in America, but it was at least lukewarm and helped take the chill from her body. She soaked the chill-clamminess from her skin and finally went back into the room, quickly getting under the covers after spreading her skirt and sweater out to dry. Under the warmth of the covers she sat up, reached over and, thanking the automatic quirk that made her take her purse from the car, she took out a comb and ran it through the copper-glint hair. Finally she lay back on the pillow, naked, pulling the sheets up around her. She would have done the same even if her bags had been there, for she'd slept in the nude ever since she was eighteen. The feel of her nakedness was both sensual and practical, the cool touch of sheets on her body a tactile sensation, and the complete freedom and sense of release a relaxing, sleep-inducing thing. Now, as she lay in the huge dark room, she frowned and tried to put aside her own dark thoughts. It had been a very different arrival from what she'd expected and more than a little upsetting. But sheer physical exhaustion flooded over the girl as she lay in the bed and closed her eyes in sleep. Yet, despite her exhaustion, she tossed and turned and glimpsed a red lantern that vanished, a tree toppling without wind or storm, and black consuming water that flowed over her. Finally she fell asleep, a deep, complete sleep.

The morning sun was an insistent intruder as it streamed through the tall windows. The girl lay half-covered by the sheet, her cream-white, high, round breasts moving in rhythm as she slept, her head a fiery halo on the pillow. Eileen woke slowly and let the room swim into focus and her mind reassemble itself. In the morning light the room was a soft beige with dark woodwork. In the full-length mirror on one wall Eileen glimpsed her beauty as she swung her long legs out of bed. Her clothes, though more than a little wrinkled, had dried out enough to wear and she dressed quickly. Before going downstairs she went to the tall windows and opened them to stand on a small balcony outside. Before her the green lawn of the great house stretched out, beyond that were rolling hills, and to the left and right, thick woods. Directly before her the tall ridge rose high, and from the window she could see the banks of red oaks that climbed up it, the red ridge from which the house had taken its name. She saw the road she'd come up on during the night and it curved out of sight where the interlocking trees came together. A thrush sang, and she saw a blackbird swoop across the grass. The land was thoroughly lush and warm and peaceful, green and inviting. Below, she saw the gaunt, cavernous-faced man, Brannock, pushing a wheelbarrow of sod. She left the window and went downstairs just as the man came in the front door. His face even more hollow-cheeked in the light of the day, his deep eyes were black, fathomless pits.

"Any word from Lady Donegan?" Eileen asked. Brannock shook his head slowly from side to side.

"I want to report my accident to the authorities and get my car from the lake if possible," the girl said. "All my things are in it. Is there a phone?"

"Just inside the library," Brannock said, gesturing to a room adjoining the living room.

Eileen kept her own glance coldly austere, reacting to the thinly disguised hostility of the man. "Where's the nearest police station?" she asked.

"In Cladvale, only a half-mile down the road," Brannock said, seeming to imply that it was far too near to waste a phone call. "But Constable Ferguson wouldn't be in this early," he added. "You can get him after ten o'clock sometime."

Eileen had started to turn for the library but halted and swung about. In that case she would walk down to the village. But not till she'd returned to the lough. She wanted to examine the scene again in the morning light. Perhaps daylight would explain what seemed inexplicable last night. She walked past Brannock, coming only to his shoulder though she was a fairly tall girl. She felt the man's eyes burning into her as she walked from the house and across the green grass of the lawn. Half-turning, she saw Brannock had followed her outside.

"If Lady Donegan returns while I'm gone, tell her I'll be back shortly," Eileen said crisply. She turned away and strode on toward the road. The garage adjoining the big house was open and she saw the two cars inside, one a small Austin, the other an older but powerful Jaguar. Brannock was crossing the lawn at an angle from her and she called out to him.

"Wouldn't Lady Donegan have taken at least one of the cars?" she asked.

"Usually," he answered. "But if she were going to get the train at Kerrydun, she might have called O'Leary's Livery Service to drive her there. Many folks do that and she'd done it before."

Eileen nodded, but the sight of the two cars sitting so quietly seemed to say something, and a grim foreboding coursed through her. It was an echo of the alarm she had felt the night before. What could have called her aunt away so suddenly, the girl asked herself. The foreboding stayed with her as she turned and started down the road, pausing to glance back at the great House of Drumroe. Its heavy wooden frame on the great fortresslike rock base looked no less formidable, no less awesome in the clean freshness of the day. The great house seemed to look down at her as though it would swallow her up in its vastness, and there was a waiting quality to it, like that of a huge beetle. Eileen turned away and went down the road with quick, firm steps, the sun turning the dark copper of her hair into a gleaming, brilliant headdress. The interlocking trees she passed under were a cool inviting tunnel now, and the land was warm and friendly. A small stream she hadn't seen last night flowed alongside the road. She rounded the bend and went onto the main road, and through a cluster of columbine she saw the blue water of the lough, calm and sparkling in the early sun. She hurried forward and was soon on the stretch of road bordering the lough. Directly ahead she saw the bank of trees and, just past them, the dead tree lying across the road. Skirting the big, lifeless tree, she went to the shallow incline of the bank. A sudden movement at the edge of the line of trees caught her eye and she turned, startled. The man, on one knee, almost at the water's edge, looked up at her from a wide strong face with gray-blue eyes that bore into her with a penetrating directness. Dark hair and dark eyebrows gave contrast to his fair skin. He wore slacks and a checked jacket over a turtle neck sweater of light beige.

"Good morning," he said and his voice was calm, quiet. "I'm sorry I startled you."

His glance took in every inch of her in one quick appraising sweep of his gray-blue eyes, Eileen noticed. His eyes were not only very direct, but they also held a cool skepticism.

"I just didn't expect to find anyone else here," Eileen said, recovering her composure. She wished she didn't look so wrinkled. The man smiled a slow, easy smile.

"I didn't expect to find anyone either, certainly no one so beautiful," he said. "I'd be guessing that makes us even then."

His speech was no thick country brogue, but it definitely had the lilt of the Irish tongue in it.

"Last night, around midnight it was, I heard a loud splash, like that of something big going into the lough, a car perhaps," he said. "I've a cottage that's just around the far bend. You can't see it from here. I came out when I heard the noise last night but the mist was so heavy I couldn't see a thing. I listened but I heard nothing else, so finally I went back in. But my curiosity was aroused, so I walked around the lough this morning. Something did happen last night. There are skid marks and tire tracks going down the bank here."

"Something happened last night, all right," Eileen said grimly. "It was my car and it went into the lake."

The man's eyebrows lifted and he got to his feet. He was bigger and broader than he'd looked down on one knee, and he came up the bank in one easy bound.

"I'm Eileen Donegan, from New York," Eileen introduced herself. "I'm Lady Donegan's niece and I was on my way to Drumroe from Shannon when it happened."

She stopped as she saw the expression of shocked surprise come over the man's face. "You're who?" he asked, frowning.

"Lady Donegan's niece from New York," Eileen said. The man recovered quickly and let a slow smile replace the expression of incredulity he'd worn. "Why does that surprise you so?" Eileen asked. His face held the slow, pleasant smile.

"I just didn't know Lady Donegan had a niece anywhere," he said smoothly. "I'm Colin Riorden." He held out his hand and she took it. His grip was firm and the gray-blue eyes were cool and skeptically appraising once again. "What made you go into the lough?" he asked. His eyes shifted to the tree across the road. "Did you swerve to avoid the tree?" he questioned almost casually.

Eileen shook her head and her full red lips grew tight. "I stopped at a red warning lantern in the road," she said. "I'd just stopped when the tree fell, all of a sudden. I tried to get away from it and I managed to avoid being flattened completely by it. But it hit the rear of the car and knocked me into the water. I almost drowned, but I was able to get out."

"I'd say you were very lucky indeed, Eileen Donegan," Colin Riorden said, his unwavering gray-blue eyes watching her, his face serious.

"Yes, but there are a number of things I don't understand at all," Eileen replied. "There was no storm, no lightning or high winds. Trees just don't fall without warning like that, without reason."

"Sometimes they might," he said quietly. "They just let go and topple, like people, you could say. It was probably in a bad way and ready to fall. You said there was a warning lantern."

"That's another thing," Eileen said with a toss of her copper hair. "When I got out of the water I rested and then came back here. The lantern was gone."

"What are you implying?" he asked and the gray-blue eyes narrowed a little though they lost none of their skepticism.

"I don't know what I'm implying," Eileen said. "But I'm saying it was a very, very strange accident."

He tossed her a wide grin. "Word games," he said softly, making her feel angrily childish. "Is there some reason why it wouldn't have been anything but an accident?"

She thought of the fear that had seized her as she drove through the night from Shannon, but she said nothing of that. "No, I guess not," she answered. "But I'm going to see the police in Cladvale about the car, at least."

"That would be Constable Ferguson," Colin Riorden said lightly.

"And I'll feel better when Lady Donegan gets back," Eileen added.

"She's away?" Colin Riorden said, interested surprise in his voice. "Wasn't she expecting you?"

"She was," Eileen answered quickly. "I'd cabled her when I'd be arriving. I came at her request—and not only did she suddenly leave yesterday, but no one seemed to expect me."

"Who told you she left yesterday?" Colin Riorden asked and there was a moment of crispness to his voice that he quickly smoothed over with an affable smile.

"Brannock, the handyman at Drumroe," Eileen replied. "It's all very strange, I'm thinking."

"More implications?" the man smiled. "They'll be wasted on Constable Ferguson."

"Why do you say that?"

"Because the Constable's idea of trouble is a poacher or a chicken thief," Colin Riorden said. "Dark and devious doings are beyond his thinking."

Eileen felt her lips tighten. She really hadn't meant to sound so dire, but her inner feelings had obviously come through. At least this big, steady, direct-eyed man had caught them all too accurately. She felt her cheeks flush with a faint glow.

"Do you know my aunt, Mr. Riorden?" Eileen asked. The slow smile reached out to her again. Only the blue-gray eyes remained steady, surveying.

"Please make that Colin," he said. "I've never cared for being called *Mister* Riorden. I've enough time for that when I get older."

She allowed herself a small smile but there was waiting in her eyes. "All right, if you like," Eileen said. "Do you know my aunt, Colin?"

"Everybody around here knows Lady Donegan of Drumroe," he said affably. Eileen's eyes narrowed a fraction. She knew of her countrymen's way of giving the impression the question had been answered when it really had been deftly sidestepped. Her mother had been excellent at it when she wanted to avoid a difficult answer. Eileen smiled, a wide, dazzling smile this time.

"Yes, but do *you* personally know her?" she said. "Have you ever met her directly?"

Colin Riorden's smile broadened and this time even the gray-blue eyes held something more than cool skepticism.

"I spoke to her only last week at Drumroe," he said quietly. "You've a bit of the bulldog in you, haven't you, lass?"

Eileen shrugged. "Perhaps," she smiled. He was a very likable person, this broad quiet man, and yet there was something held back about him, as though his pleasant affability was a kind of cloak for something else. "What do you do here in this lovely countryside?" she asked casually.

"I'm an historian," he answered. "I'm studying the history of the major families of Ireland and their influence on local, regional, and national attitudes. I've a grant from Trinity College in Dublin and I've been in my little rented cottage here for some six months now. It's really very pleasant and snug."

"And your work is what brought you in contact with my aunt?" Eileen questioned.

"Indeed it was," Colin Riorden said, letting his eyes sweep the blue water of the lough. "A fine morning it is," he said, putting his hands into his trouser pockets. "You say Lady Donegan left no word about where she might have gone or when she'd be back?"

"None at all," Eileen said.

"Well, I'd better get back to doing some work this fine day," Colin Riorden said cheerfully. "You must stop in and visit me sometime. My cottage is the only one fronting directly on the lough. Will you be staying on a while?"

"I don't really know," Eileen answered.

"I guess you'll know better about that after you talk with Lady Donegan," he smiled at her. "She'll have some good reason for going off so suddenly. There's a rational explanation for everything, isn't there?"

"No!" Eileen said, snapping the word out more forcefully than she had intended to do. Colin Riorden's eyes almost twinkled at her and he nodded again and walked off down the road. She watched him go, a big, broad-shouldered figure. He had a highly effective way of casually slipping questions into a conversation, she realized as she watched him disappear around the bend. In a half minute he'd extracted from her the information that Aunt Agnes had left no word for her at all, that she didn't know how long she'd be here and that she was highly skeptical of some rational explanations. Was it only the way of an historian accustomed to probing into things? Or was it something else? It was too damned effective, whatever it was, she told herself in annoyance.

Eileen turned and walked over to where the old tree blocked the road. She knelt to examine the base of it, the dead, twisted roots. They were indeed dry, withered, useless as roots. Yet they would serve well enough to anchor the lifeless old tree, she told herself, and she examined the ground where the tree had stood. She couldn't be sure, but it seemed unusually torn up for having just pulled out of the ground. It seemed as though the ground had been dug out around the few roots still imbedded there so the slightest push could topple the tree. Rising to her feet, she knew only that she didn't really know anything for certain. But there were still unexplained things here, and a lantern that had just up and vanished. She thought again of Colin Riorden and the shock in his face when she told him who she was. Had he been surprised to see her because he expected she was inside the car at the bottom of the lake? She took a deep breath and held it for a second, letting it out finally in a loud rush of air. She had no right to think such things about the pleasant, direct-eyed man she had only just met. She had the Irish hatred of injustice born into her and that's what she was doing now, being unjust, and she was ashamed of herself for it. There had really been something very reassuringly steady about him, she reflected as she walked on, and she vowed to set aside unfounded imaginings for the time being. But the foreboding inside her would stay, she knew, smoldering there until it flared up into demanding flame or was answered in some way.

Eileen passed the grim house as she walked back toward the village of Cladvale. Brannock, trimming a hedge, looked up as she passed but he made no sign that her aunt had returned, and so Eileen kept on. The road wound its way downward, bordered by blue gentians, and the sun had grown warmer, bathing the countryside in a soft, peaceful glow. She was almost ashamed of the suspicions that had churned about inside her. Around a bend she paused to watch a farmer rethatching the roof of his cottage. He had already taken off the old straw and was just finishing a layer of *marl*, the soft yellowish clay that forms a base for the new straw. The long willow strips that would bind the new straw to the roof were hanging from one end of the cottage, she saw. Moving on as the man continued with his careful work, Eileen walked down the road until, with a magical suddenness, the village of Cladvale appeared in front of her, low houses of blue-white limestone, wood and slate roofs on some, thatched roofs on others, a few of fieldstone, knobby and full of character. The village was really a winding continuation of the road with a double row of houses on either side of it. In the center Eileen saw the modest spire of the kirk. There were elderly women in shawls, a few young largeboned girls, tradesmen and merchants, and she caught their curious glances as she walked down the street. She was as yet a *gal*, or stranger, here, but she remembered enough of her childhood to know that it wouldn't take long before every soul in Cladvale would know who she was.

A curious-eyed old man with a crate of chickens told her where to find the Constable, and she followed a small path a few doors off the main street. The doorway of a small house was simply marked CONSTABLE and she entered a neat, compact office. A young man, somewhat heavy faced, sat at a small table to one side and as she entered, glanced up from a ledger book of some sort. Constable Ferguson was seated at a desk, and he got up. He was elderly, stooped, and weathered, wearing a tweed jacket with leather patches on the elbows. She introduced herself to the accompaniment of raised eyebrows, and after Constable Ferguson listened to her tell what had happened, he murmured sympathies and got right to the matter at hand.

"I'll have to call Kerrydun," he said, more to himself than her. "Jim O'Brien has a big tractor with a chain rig there. We'll have to fish for the car, I'm thinking. And I'll have the Dolan boys get that tree off the road right away."

"What about that tree, Constable?" Eileen asked. "What about the strange way it suddenly fell like that?"

"It's a wondrous thing you weren't killed," he said, frowning with sincerity. "Wondrous, indeed."

"I thought so myself," she said tartly. "And what about the red lantern?"

"You just didn't find it, lass," he said. "It'll turn up." He reached into a drawer and brought out a long-stemmed pipe, which he stuck into his mouth unlighted. Looking over it at Eileen, he sat back in the chair. "So you're the Lady Donegan's niece from America," he said. "We'll see to it you get back all your things, don't you worry. At least we'll know where to find you, won't we?"

Eileen forced a smile and Colin Riorden's words rang mockingly in her mind. "Yes, I'll be at Drumroe," she said. "Thank you for your help."

She left Constable Ferguson with a pleased, slightly smug expression on his face, though the red-faced younger man at the side table seemed to glare at her with hostility. As she went back to the main street and turned right, she frowned inwardly at the cold look in his eyes. A sign had caught her eye as she'd started up to the Constable's office, and now she walked over to the small garage that stood open under the sign, O'LEARY'S LIVERY

SERVICE. An old, high-bodied Morris sedan took up the front section of the garage, and a two-wheeled road cart the rest. A young man in overalls and a blue shirt looked up from the cart as she entered. He was aware at once that she was not a girl from a nearby village or even another county. She was as beautiful as any colleen he'd ever seen, but there was something else to her, a way of walking, an independent, commanding look to her that was the mark of another land. He came forward at once.

"Mr. O'Leary?" she said, and he noticed the way the sun streaming in the door sent copper shafts glinting from her hair.

"No, Mr. O'Leary's out at the moment," the young man said. "Could I be helping you?"

"Perhaps," Eileen smiled. "My aunt, Lady Donegan, was apparently called away unexpectedly. Did she call on your service to drive her to Kerrydun or anywhere else?"

"No, she didn't," the man said. "I'd know. I do most of the driving myself and all of it outside the immediate area. Ever since Mr. O'Leary's rheumatism got bad, he only takes the short trips nearby."

"You're sure, then, Lady Donegan didn't use your service in the last few days," Eileen repeated.

"Positive, ma'am," the young man answered. Eileen nodded a thank-you at him and hurried from the little garage. As she walked quickly from the village back toward the great house, the foreboding inside her grew deeper, more chilling. Something was wrong, very wrong here at Drumroe. Aunt Agnes knew she was coming and had simply gone off. Why? It didn't make sense, not any more sense than trees that suddenly toppled and red lanterns that vanished. If there were answers to be uncovered, they wouldn't be found by Constable Ferguson, and once again she thought of Colin Riorden and saw his blue-gray eyes with their cool skepticism. He had been so quick at picking up the tones of her remarks. Perhaps he'd be helpful in other ways. By the time she reached the house she'd made one decision. If Aunt

Agnes didn't return by that evening, she'd pay Colin Riorden a visit. He was studying the history of the people of this area and he'd spoken to Aunt Agnes only last week. Perhaps he could remember something helpful if she prodded him. She entered the front door of the big house. She was annoyed at herself. She didn't like alarmists and she hated being one, but once again she was caught up by something beyond herself, inner voices, silent certainties demanding obeisance. She feared them, and she feared what they insistently whispered to her. She wouldn't listen, she told herself. This time they were wrong. She opened the big door and went inside.

CHAPTER THREE

BRANNOCK WAS in the hallway polishing the dark woodwork when she entered, his cadaverous face as expressionless as ever.

"No word from Lady Donegan, I take it," Eileen said.

"No word," he replied with his steel-file voice. Eileen grimaced silently. She was about to go up the stairs when she felt her stomach rumble, and she suddenly realized that, among all other things, she was hungry.

"Where is the kitchen?" she asked, and Brannock pointed down to the end of the hallway.

"Cook will be back today," he said. "She left Monday night, sudden sickness in the family."

Everyone seemed to have taken off, Eileen said to herself with a wry grimness. As she went down the hall, she paused for a moment to look into the large library with its book-lined walls and leather sofa and chairs. She remembered the room. As a little girl it had impressed her the most with its heavy, overpowering size and dark woodwork. Even now, despite the books which normally impart a certain warmth to a room, it had an air of formal severity, as though its riches were to be approached with awe rather than enthusiasm. She went down the hall and found the kitchen to be big and old-fashioned, a place of old, heavy stoves, iron kettles, and thick wooden cabinets. But, despite that, it had a warmth to it, a sense of security, and the feel of a place used to turning out good, hearty meals. She found cups and a series of well-stocked cupboards, but not the one thing she desperately yearned for—coffee. That was one thing she had become most American in, a love for a good cup of coffee. But here she found tea leaves, powdered tea, Indian tea, English tea and Irish tea, but no coffee. "Not even a damned tea bag," Eileen muttered as she poured the tea leaves into a tea pot and put a kettle of water on the old stove. Finally she found some wonderfully filling, tasty Irish soda bread and jam to have with the tea she brewed. She had just finished and cleared away the dishes when she heard the sound of a car coming to a halt outside. She ran up the hall to the front door and pulled it open.

A tall, rangy man was just unfolding from a small open-topped MG. He wore a dark brown suit and his sandy hair half-fell over his forehead. His eyes, when they turned on her, were china blue, and his smile had a rakish tightness to it that made her sorry once again she looked so wrinkled.

"Well, now, I'd be saying that the good villagers of Cladvale left out something," he said, and his tongue had more of the lilt of the land to it than Colin Riorden's had. He came toward her and smiled down at her with a commanding charm that made itself felt at once.

"I'm Rory Muldoon, Lady Donegan's solicitor," he said, and Eileen felt a flood of relief go through her. Here, at last, was someone who could help unravel things, perhaps.

"Am I glad to see you, Mr. Muldoon," she said.

"That's good," he laughed. "They told me in town that a niece of Lady Donegan's had been there. They didn't say a strikingly beautiful niece, though. A great oversight on their part."

Eileen smiled back at him and held the door open wider.

"Please come in, there are so many questions I have for you," she said.

"I hope I've the answers," he laughed. "Let's go into the library and talk there. It's a nice, comfortable room."

He walked on ahead of her, and she realized he probably knew Drumroe a great deal better than most people. There was a controlled tautness to the man, and his quick flashing smile circled around her like an embrace. "There was something about an accident by the lough?" he asked as they went into the big, imposing room. News travelled quickly, as quickly as she'd imagined it would, she thought.

"Yes, my car went into the lough," she said. "I'd like to discuss that with you, too. But first I want to ask about my aunt. She wasn't here when I arrived. Brannock told me she apparently left suddenly, while he was in town. But she was expecting me. I just can't understand her leaving like that, without any message or word. Did she tell you where she was going?"

Rory Muldoon frowned a moment and then smiled at Eileen again, a wide, reassuring smile. "No, she didn't," he said. "But your aunt is a very independent woman."

"I am sure, but I still say it's more than a little odd," Eileen replied. "She'd written me to come and I'd cabled her when I'd be arriving. It just doesn't seem she would leave and not be here to meet me. Frankly, I'm very worried about it."

She looked up to see Rory Muldoon's china blue eyes studying her, almost boring into her. As her glance met his, his eyes softened at once and he smiled again, that quick tight smile that had the flash of sunlight in it.

"Suppose you don't be worrying yourself," he said. "Lady Donegan often goes away suddenly like that. She's a woman with many unusual ways about her. Having you come over here to sign those papers is one of them."

Eileen frowned. Aunt Agnes's letter had said that her solicitor had been adamant that she come over to sign in person.

"I understood you wanted me here to sign," the girl said.

"Oh, indeed, if that's the way it had to be," Rory Muldoon smiled at her. "But I was against your signing them in the first place. I felt then, and I still do, that the old place ought just to be let go, to the government if they want it. Once the family has run out, that's all there is. It's finished. I didn't even know you existed until your aunt brought your name up a few weeks back."

His eyes twinkled as he spoke to her, but they didn't undercut the seriousness of his voice. "As I said to Lady Donegan, why would a young girl want to rattle around in an old place like this?" he went on. "Especially a young girl who's really an American now, who's used to more comforts and conveniences than we know exist here. And then, of course, the problem of taxes, of maintenance, of help are really substantial. But your aunt insisted that the choice of what happens to Drumroe after she's gone should rightfully be yours, so she sent for you. Of course, then, I insisted you sign any papers in person here."

He smiled at her and his eyes roamed across the deep copper of her hair. "Of course, if I'd known what you looked like I'd never have tried to talk Lady Donegan out of bringing you here," he said. Eileen laughed. It was the first time she'd laughed since she arrived here. He had the vaunted charm of the Irish in more than ample measure, she decided. And it was warming and good to hear, she also decided.

"I still say this is no place for a beautiful girl like yourself to be living," he said.

"I think I agree with you there," Eileen said, glancing around at the huge room. "But what of the value of Drumroe? It must be worth a great deal. I'm sure my aunt feels she is handing on something of real value."

"Lady Donegan is handing on a tradition and not much else," he said. "Places like this are a terrible drag on the market, more bother than they're worth these days. The government might take it, and then only if they felt it was of historic value. I don't think they'll feel that way about Drumroe. Any history of Drumroe wouldn't be one they'd want to preserve, I'm thinking."

Eileen glanced at the tall, rangy man, but he didn't amplify the remark and she decided not to press him at the moment.

"But Aunt Agnes wanted me to sign the necessary papers, so I presume she had her own good reasons," Eileen said. "Possibly she felt I should be legally responsible to dispose of Drumroe, if nothing else."

"To my way of thinking that's not even necessary. It might even be a terrible burden on you," Rory Muldoon said.

"I do wish she'd get back or I'd hear from her," Eileen said. "I'd feel so much better about everything." She didn't mention the insistent foreboding. How do you explain things you can't explain to yourself?

Rory Muldoon stood up. "Look, I've a grand idea," he said, his eyes laughing. "There are such a lot of pros and cons on this thing. Why don't you have dinner with me tonight and I'll go over everything with you in detail. Besides, you're the loveliest thing that these old eyes have seen in a long time."

Eileen brushed back her copper hair. She liked the idea at once. Dinner with this charming, tautly strung man would be a welcome change from what her visit had been thus far. But she looked down at herself with dismay.

"I'd love to, really I would," she said. "I want to talk to you more about that accident, for one thing. But I'm not dressed for going out anywhere. All my things are still at the bottom of the lough."

"There's a very nice shop in Kilmor, only a half-hour or so past Cladvale," he said. "You've all afternoon to get there and back."

"I could buy some new things," she mused aloud, taking to the idea at once. "Even when they're fished from the water, my things will take days to dry out. All right, Mr. Muldoon, we've a dinner date."

"Rory, please," he smiled at her. "I'll pick you up here at six. Ireland's still not a land for late dining."

She watched him go from the door, a light springy step to his walk. When she turned away she felt that she had at last found a friend, someone to help her. But she thought instantly of Aunt Agnes's continued absense and the chill inside her leaped up at once. Despite Rory Muldoon's words, she was increasingly worried. Something was wrong, terribly wrong. She heard a door open and Brannock came up a flight of steps from the cellar.

"I'm going to take one of the cars," she said to the gaunt-faced, dour man. "I'll be back later this afternoon."

"It's Lady Donegan's place to give permission for use of the cars," he said sourly, and Eileen saw the hostility in his deep eyes. She felt her temper rise and she decided to strike back at once.

"First of all, Brannock, Lady Donegan's not here to give permission," she said crisply. "Second, I'm here at her invitation, so I doubt she'd deny me permission. And third, if anything has happened to Lady Donegan, I will be the new mistress of Drumroe."

She watched the message sink in as Brannock slowly turned away and went outside. She followed him out, crossing to the garage, and she was glad he couldn't see her hands trembling. The man frightened her, despite her pose of defiance. There was something sinister about him, a waiting watchfulness that had its own ominousness about it. In between the garage and the house there was a narrow passageway, and Eileen looked down it and out to the rear of the great house. She saw what appeared to be a small vegetable garden and beyond that, on a distant hillock, a cleared area of at least a dozen or so headstones, a small cemetery. It was an entirely unexpected sight, and she frowned as she walked into the garage. She'd ask about it tonight, she told herself.

She took the powerful old Jaguar, half-smiling to herself as she did so. It imparted a feeling of power and security which she obviously needed. The keys were in both cars, in the ignition of the small Austin and over the visor of the Jaguar. She turned the engine on and heard its powerful throb. She drove from the garage, turning onto the road to Cladvale and quickly passing through the village onto a wider road. Farmers plowing a field, others gathering hay, an old man with a flock of sheep, these and other peaceful, happy scenes passed in front of her as she drove slowly. This was the land she had so eagerly wanted to come back to, a place to regenerate, to find her roots, those old truths that would give a new meaning to her life. But so far she had found only chilling fears, strange unexplained accidents, and more hostility than warmth. Yet there was peace and warmth in this land. Her eyes told her that. Her ears, hearing the sounds of laughter as she drove past the farms and travelers on foot, told her that. Her own inner certainty told her that. But so far, that peace and laughter had eluded her. Perhaps the House of Drumroe had never been a place for laughter and warmth. Perhaps there was more reason than she knew for the severe, forbidding starkness of it. Little bits of remembered history came back to her, and she shivered as she drove through the warm sunlight. Angrily, she cast aside memory. She'd forget everything except getting some new things for her dinner date. It even sounded strange. It had been some while since she'd gone out on a dinner date. After Chuck she hadn't felt like dating, and hadn't met anyone worthwhile or interesting enough. Mostly, though, it had been a reaction, she knew, to Chuck, to her own loneliness, to fear of making mistakes again. But now she looked forward to it as a welcome change. She stepped on the gas pedal and the big, heavy car moved forward faster until her hair flowed out behind her, a trail of flame.

Kilmor was not much larger than Cladvale but, because it stood at the intersection of the main road to Ulster and to Fermanagh it received a stream of through traffic that was reflected in its shops. Eileen found the small dress shop easily enough. The tweeds and silks were particularly lovely, though hardly high fashion. But a few pins and a scissor could do wonders, and when she left the store the rear seat of the car was piled high with boxes and there was a song in her heart, a small song at least.

The drive back was pleasant and cool as the afternoon sun began to set. Backing the car into the garage, she took her purchases into the big house with her. She was halfway up the stairs when she heard her name.

"Miss Donegan," she heard a woman's voice call from below and she turned to see a short, plump round-faced woman standing in the foyer. She wore a flowered print dress and a white apron over it. "I'm Molly McConnell," the woman said. "I'm Lady Donegan's cook. I'm sorry I wasn't here to welcome you when you arrived."

Eileen put her things on the steps and went down to where the plump little woman waited. She had kind merry eyes, Eileen saw, in a pleasant open face.

"Lord but you're a beautiful one, you are," the woman said as Eileen came down to her. "Is Lady Donegan in town?"

"Lady Donegan wasn't here when I arrived," Eileen said. "I was just about to ask you if you knew where she might have gone."

The cook's round face clouded as she frowned in thought. "She was here when I was called away to go to my sister's bedside," the woman said. "That was Monday night. She'd gotten your cable. She showed it to me. She was looking forward to seeing you. There was no talk at all of her going anyplace."

Eileen held down the fear that surged up inside her at once. Molly McConnell's words had confirmed one thing, at least. Aunt Agnes had indeed expected her and wanted to be on hand to greet her. Something very unusual must have occurred to make her leave so suddenly.

"Nobody seems to know exactly when she went away or where she went," Eileen said. "Frankly, I'm worried. Mr. Muldoon was here this morning. She hadn't said anything to him, either."

"It's not like Lady Donegan at all," the cook said. "Not at all. She just doesn't go off like that, and I've been with her near ten years now."

Eileen felt her brow furrow at once. Rory Muldoon had said her aunt often went away on sudden trips. She'd bring that up again at dinner, that was certain.

"I don't understand it at all," the cook was saying. "It's not like her not to be here to welcome you."

Eileen smiled at the little woman and was warmed by the concern in her voice, the only real concern for her aunt she had met so far. Even Rory Muldoon seemed to take her absence lightly. "I'm going to be having dinner out tonight with Mr. Muldoon," Eileen said to the little woman. "There are a number of legal things to discuss. After all, that's why Lady Donegan wanted me to come."

"I know," Molly McConnell said. "Lady Donegan, God love her, used to confide in me, I'm proud to say. She's been more and more worried, getting more and more depressed."

"Over what, Molly?" Eileen probed quickly.

"New troubles bringing back old ones, she said to me," the cook answered. "It seemed to really prey on her from the time her young brother, Terence, was killed in that fall from the building in London three months ago."

Dimly, Eileen recalled getting a note in the mail of that, but she'd been too deep in her own troubles then to care about much else.

"It's good to have you here, Miss Eileen," the cook said. "It's good to have a young pretty colleen in the house. Tomorrow night I'll make you something special for dinner."

"Wonderful, Molly," the girl said. "I'd best get up and get myself ready."

She turned and hurried up the stairs, pausing to pick up the boxes she'd left on the steps. In the room that had become hers for the moment she undressed quickly and slipped into the bathtub, once again wishing for really hot water. She bathed her long, supple body and dried herself off outside beside the bed, pausing to look at herself in the full-length mirror. She was pleased at the firm, high line of her breasts, the small curve of her stomach. She put on fresh panties, and a bra that was made in America. Over it she slipped on the black dress that was the most chic item in the store. Leaving the top buttons of the neckline open gave it more verve than it really had. Six o'clock came quickly and Rory Muldoon was prompt. She was sure he would be. In the open-topped little MG they drove to another town, on the shore, to a small inn with a quaint dining room. From the window she could see the cliffs of the land, abrupt against the sea. It was a snug place, family owned, and the chill of the night outside was softened by a fire in a large stone hearth. Over the candlelit table Rory Muldoon was a charming, witty and attentive dinner companion. He was one of those men who focused all his attention on a woman, making her feel complete and totally desirable. The candle light gave his eyes a somewhat eerie but fascinating opaque quality and he kept her busy with questions about America, questions about herself, and questions about her plans for the future. On the last catagory she had few answers for him.

It was when they were having brandies after dinner that she told him about the strange accident at the edge of the lough and how she'd almost been killed there.

"Between that and Aunt Agnes's sudden disappearance, I'm beginning to wonder just what's going on around here," Eileen said. "In fact, I keep wondering if what happened to me really was an accident."

She stopped, shocked herself to hear the thought given voice at last. She hadn't wanted to sound melodramatic, but it was the way she felt.

"Maybe it wasn't an accident," Rory said, and Eileen felt her eyes widen. His hand closed over hers and she didn't draw away. It felt good, reassuring.

"You mean, someone wanted to kill me?" she gasped. "But why? There's no reason. I'd only landed here a few hours before."

"I didn't say that," he said. "I merely said maybe it wasn't an accident." Eileen's mind raced.

"You mean it wasn't aimed at me?" she asked. He nodded gravely.

"These are bad times here," he said. "Old hates have come to life again with a vengeance. It's history coming around again. It's 1916 all over again, but this time there'll be another ending."

"1916," Eileen echoed. "You mean the time of the trouble?" Automatically, she had used the colloquial way of referring to Ireland's bloody uprising for independence against the English. The uprising had started with the Easter Rebellion in 1916, been crushed and then rose up again in violent, bloody fury through to 1921. It was a time when Irishman fought Irishman, when English excesses and Irish fury competed in blood, a time when scars went deep into the land and its people. She'd heard her mother speak of it, read stories, and heard tales even as a little girl.

"Surely you've heard of the trouble going on now in Ulster," Rory Muldoon said. "It's oppression again, a new kind, that's all."

"Yes, I've heard," Eileen said. "Three thousand miles away I heard. It made all the newspapers, the fighting between Protestants and Catholics, squabbling like dogs, scratching at each other like so many animals. It almost made me ashamed to be Irish."

She saw Rory smile, but she felt the smile didn't go very deep. "You've been away too long to feel it," he said softly. "You've been separated too long from the roots of the land."

"I've been separated long enough to see that there's nothing to be gained by keeping old hatreds alive. Distance lends a sense of perspective to things."

He smiled again. "There are many here who say Ireland will never be free until it's one country," he said. "What's been going on in Ulster tends to prove they're right. But I'm not at all sure that it's just distance that's speaking in you, Eileen Donegan."

"And pray tell, what does that mean?" Eileen shot back.

"The house of Drumroe has a history of not agreeing with the times," he smiled. "It could be in your blood."

"Oh, come now, Rory, you're a solicitor, a lawyer, an educated man," she said. "You don't believe in the inheritance of good ideas and bad ideas, of goodness and evil."

"I'm educated enough to know what we don't know," he answered. "Every day we find more things that the genes inherit, that are passed on. Today it's fashionable to say that evil is something that man does. But maybe it's something that man is. We know that whole families can carry a disease of the blood or an imbalance of chromosomes. Why not, then, a disease of the mind or the spirit? If the capacity for intelligence can be inherited, and no one casts doubt on that, why not the capacity for evil? An interesting question, now, isn't it?"

He was smiling at her, but once again she wondered how deep the smile went. "All right, it is that," she said. "But where does it fit in with what happened to me at the lough?"

"Only that today the land is filled with special agents, police, Ulstermen, undercover spies," he said. "Because we're so close to Ulster here in Donegal, the tension and activity is greater than anywhere else. There's plenty of arms smuggling going on across the border these nights and plenty of secret preparations being made. And there are plenty of agents about trying to uncover what's going on. It's entirely possible that a trap had been set up for someone who was to pass along that road. There was a last-minute change in plans, and instead you came along and were mistaken for whoever was to be there."

Eileen sat back with a sense of shock. "It's absolutely unbelievable," she said. "But it does make some sense out of what happened last night, I must admit."

She looked at Rory Muldoon and saw him studying her closely. "But it doesn't explain why Aunt Agnes just up and left so suddenly," she said. "Why did you tell me she often did that, Rory? Molly McConnell said it wasn't like her at all."

"Molly McConnell has an overactive mouth," he said and smiled quickly, softening the reply at once. "I told you that because I thought it would stop you from worrying so much."

Eileen put her hand on his in instant reaction, feeling the flood of warm gratefulness sweep over her. "I'm sorry, Rory," she said. "I should have guessed as much."

His other hand came down over hers, and she felt the strength of his fingers on her arm. She saw his eyes flick to where the round swell of her breasts rose up from the unbuttoned neck of the dress.

"This is no place for you right now, Eileen," he said. "That's why I wanted your aunt to forget about your signing those papers and forget about Drumroe. But she's a woman of strange convictions."

"Why will signing hurt me?" Eileen asked.

"If you sign the papers and, God forbid, Lady Donegan passes on, you are legally responsible for Drumroe, of course," he said, keeping his grip on her arm. "But you know that much now. What you don't realize is that it's not just going to be a matter of signing off an old house. The government could take months, maybe a year, to decide about taking over Drumroe. Frankly, I doubt that they will. Meanwhile, you'd be responsible for the upkeep of it, the taxes on it, the help and maintenance of it as a place in good condition. It could become a terrible burden on you. You would find yourself involved in ways you never dreamed of being involved."

"And if I don't sign, if I just pick up and go?"

"The place would stand when Lady Donegan died and no one could be charged with legal responsibility. It would be up to the government to take it on or not, and anything that happened to it while they wrestled with the decision would be their problem."

Eileen felt her eyes held by the power of his intense, searching look. "I'd say go home, forget Drumroe, especially now," he said. "Drumroe was involved before in troubled times. Let it not be again. It's more than advice I'm giving you, Eileen, it's the lessons of history."

"You speak in parables of sorts, Rory," Eileen laughed. "I think I'd better get back now. You've certainly given me a lot to think about."

"I hope so," he smiled, standing up. "If you go back, I'd have the chance to see you again, in America, under better conditions. So you see, I'm really being selfish."

She linked her arm into his and looked up at the tallness of him, the sandy boyish hair falling down over his forehead. "I'd like that," she said. "I really would. But I've got to think some more, Rory. And I'd want to talk to Aunt Agnes, first. All this talk of trouble, and the fighting that's been going on, it depresses me so much. I think it's terrible, really terrible. I think there ought to be a better way to work out differences."

"What you think doesn't really matter," Rory said. "What the people think is what matters."

His words dug into her, but then she realized that he wasn't being biting. It was only the truth he had said. He was really very nice, she told herself. But, then, she'd already decided that.

When they reached Drumroe, the little car halted in the depths of the black shadows alongside the front of the big house. She heard the laughter in his voice as he helped her out of the car.

"I've heard that in America it's thought bad manners not to kiss a girl good night, even on the first meeting," he said, and before she could answer his lips were on hers. His kiss was surprisingly insistent and his hands pressed into the soft swell at the top of her breasts. She had just begun to feel the warm stir of desire when he stepped back. "That's just so you don't think me impolite," he said.

He was in the car a moment later. "Think on what I've said to you, Eileen. Think carefully on it."

She went in, faintly troubled by the almost-warning tone of his last words. Perhaps he was being overly dire in an effort to impress her. No matter, she was warmly grateful for his interest and concern. It had been, all in all, a very nice, very needed evening. There was a note on the small table in the hall at the foot of the stairs. It was Molly McConnell telling her there'd been no word from Lady Donegan. Eileen felt the chill inside her at once, and she almost went to speak to the cook, but she decided there was really nothing to be gained at this late hour. When she went into her room and turned on the light, she found her bags strewn about, unpacked, and the contents spread out to dry. Her clothes hung from a variety of hangers all over the room, some things folded across the backs of chairs to dry. She smiled and made a mental note to thank Molly in the morning. The car had been salvaged from the lough, obviously, and was no doubt someplace in Cladvale, probably outside O'Leary's Livery Service.

She undressed and lay naked across the bed with only a sheet tossed casually over her long, slender form. A glance at her watch told her it really wasn't that late. It only seemed so here in this quiet land where the night was a time for sleeping or staying safely indoors. Her mind was a jumble of thoughts as she lay there and once again heard the things Rory had said to her. They were disturbing, but not nearly so disturbing as the gnawing fear that possessed her, the same inner sense of alarm she'd had when she drove from the airport to the House of Drumroe. In the morning she would visit Colin Riorden, she decided. Perhaps he would have a helpful idea or two. Rory, for all his being Aunt Agnes's solicitor, seemed to know little more than she did about her aunt's movements. But he did know about the troubles and tensions in the land, and his talk of uprisings and independence made her recall all those tales she'd heard as a child and the things she had studied in college. In addition, there was a kind of memory that was more then memory inside her. It welled up from her subconscious, a recollection of moods and feelings, a kind of empathy that transcended mere memory and mere learning. She thought of Rory's words about what we have the capacity to inherit, intelligence, evil, and she wondered. Could we perhaps inherit powers which we refuse to admit because we cannot yet understand them? Could we inherit a sense of psychic empathy or, and she felt her hands tighten, the ability to receive psychic messages, flashes of knowledge beyond our present ability to explain? Eileen felt a coldness sweep over her and she pulled the sheet tighter around her nakedness. If those things were possible, were those people given it blessed with good or evil? Or, as she had sometimes felt, doomed to live with a terrible burden, an ability to see when one didn't want to see, to know when one didn't want to know? The possibilities were staggering and, especially to her, terribly frightening.

The girl got up and walked to a chair where her light robe had been spread out to dry. The cold and wet had gone from it, so she slipped it on and went to the tall windows to look out. The line of the ridge was directly ahead of her, clear and sharp, rising over the night mists that drifted across the ground below. Out there in the blackness, according to Rory Muldoon, men were moving through the night, living echoes of fifty years ago, preparing to shed Irish blood again on Irish land and start another cycle of pain and hate. Once again emotions and not reason would rule. Once again old wrongs would be used to justify new ones. Once again the mistakes of religious men and not the meaning of religion would be used as a rallying point. But this time there was a tragic difference. This time there were none of the great ones who had given form and mind to the rebellion of 1916. This time there was no O'Casey, no Joyce, Yeats or Synge to give meaning to the blood that was being shed. They weren't here because the world had changed, and the trouble now was not really the same, not here, at least. Now the trouble was more of an infection of unrest, the anarchy that was sweeping the world. Only here, in Ireland, the old hatreds, the old wounds, had never been let to die, and it was easy to open them up again. But then, it was always easier to fight than to think.

Eileen found herself frowning as she listened to her own thoughts, frowning at the depth of her convictions. She hadn't even really thought much about it before now and suddenly, back here in the land of her birth, it was as if she had to take a stand, to hold fast to what she believed. Rory had said that Lady Donegan was a "woman of strange convictions." Eileen smiled. Perhaps she, too, was a woman of strange convictions. Damn, she said aloud, that heredity business again. But then perhaps it wasn't so strange at all. This was a land of strange convictions and strange beliefs, but they were only strange because they couldn't be explained in cold, rational terms. She had come back here to find herself, to find herself so she could start over again, and maybe she was doing that, merely in a way she hadn't expected.

She started to turn away from the tall windows when she saw the large, silver sphere come up beyond the ridge, moving slowly into view, casting its cold light out before it. It was a three-quarter-full moon and it rose into the sky over the top of the ridge as she watched it. Then, coming through the night like the cry of a lonely lover, she heard the sound of the fife. Soft, yet crystal clear it was, and as she heard the slow cadenced song of the fife she felt her lips forming the words of it, words that rose up from the depths of her mind, words she'd known long ago and had heard but a few, infrequent times since then. But now they came back to her, slowly at first, but spurred by the sound of the fife.

"O come tell me, Shaun O'Farrell,
   Tell me why you hurry so,
Hush you look and hush you listen,
   And his cheeks were all aglow."

The high, plaintive, and softly wild notes of the fife drifted into the room as she opened the window and she heard the sound of their call.

"I've got orders from the captain,
    Make you quick and ready soon,
For the pikes must be together,
    By the risin' of the moon.

"By the risin' of the moon,
    By the risin' of the moon ....
The pikes must be together,
    By the risin' of the moon."

The ancient song of rebellion, calling the men from the towns and the hills, a call come down through the centuries, sounded in 1798, 1848, 1916, and 1918, and times enough in between those major uprisings. It had called names now written into the land: Wolfe Tone, Father Murphy, Robert Emmet, O'Donovan, Rossa and Kevin Barry, Roger Casement, and Charles Steward Parnell. Now it called her for different reasons, but it called nonetheless. Eileen felt the pair of jeans on the hangar. The hard fabric had dried already and so had a checked cotton shirt hanging nearby. She slipped on the clothes while the sound of the fife still hung in the night. She had to see for herself. So far she had listened only to words, some monosyllabic, some noncommittal, some well-intentioned, but still only words. She wanted to see for herself. Was what Rory Muldoon had told her really so, or was this but a lone fife player in the night? Were there really men moving through the night once again, preparing for bloodshed, gathering in secret to plot? Or were there but a few youths playing at games their father's lived? She had to know, to be sure. It would help her decide what to do about Drumroe. It would tell her whether Rory Muldoon was overreacting himself, exaggerating for his own reasons.

She hurried from the room and flew down the dark steps, not thinking about a fall that could break her neck. Outside in the night, she ran across the lawn toward the ridge, toward the sound of the fife. She would see what she could learn by the rising of the moon. The mists, not so heavy as the other night, still made waving, clutching hands of the trees as she started up the ridge. The sound of the fife was distant now and coming from the right. She turned, away from the ridge, and started up the steep mountain that formed the right end of the ridge line. The mists were not so thick here, but the thorns and brushes grabbed at her legs as she climbed. She could still hear the fife, but it was a thin sound now and she hurried her steps, falling, getting up at once to press on. But the sound was wavering now, caught by the soft winds and tossed from the hills and rises of the mountain, coming from one place and then from another. Eileen hurried on. Then it faded away, came back again for a brief moment, and then left once more.

"Damn!" Eileen said, pausing. "I've lost it." She glanced around in the blackness, the moon a white ball through the trees. She couldn't see the way she had come. She'd run faster and farther than she'd realized. Retracing her steps would take more than a little doing. She'd come a good ways up into the mountain and, with honesty, she hadn't any idea where she was. She'd started for the ridge and then turned right to go up the mountainside, but that was all she remembered. It had been a foolish thing, an impulsive gesture, but it had been triggered by a desire to get at the truth of something, anything. Aunt Agnes was missing; there was still no explanation of why she'd left. The incident with the car and the lough had possibly been explained by Rory, and yet it wasn't fact. But the fife had been a chance to pin something down. Eileen frowned as suddenly she wondered again why it was so important to her to know whether the land was filled with rebellion. But then why had her own convictions so crystallized since she had come to Drumroe? Was it all part of finding herself? Was it all a purging before the peace? Purging! It was a word she disliked. It smacked of superstitions and people burned as witches, and sent chills through her. Yet she had used it just now herself. Why? Because it was the right word, because there was something inside her that had to be purged out before she could find herself?

Eileen turned and started down the mountainside, suddenly steeper than it had seemed on her way up. She went on aimlessly, wandering a hundred yards till she saw a light flickering in the distance, the soft light of a campfire's glow. It was on her level, but half-way around the side of the mountain. Yet campers would probably know how to help her find her way back. She moved toward the light, pulling herself along on the tree branches, using rocks to rest on. The light, blocked out by clusters of trees from time to time, continued to flicker and grow brighter as she neared. The mists had risen, and she realized that her footsteps had taken her slightly downward, too. The glow began to shape itself as she neared and Eileen halted, frowning. It was no small campfire's light, but a long, thin shaft of fire, like that of a tall log being burned. Eileen crept forward carefully, skirting the rocks that had started to take the place of trees as the mountainside turned craggy and full of boulders. The long thin flame grew more pronounced and she saw that it was indeed a tall log burning, and in front of it figures moved in and out of the flickering light. Eileen moved through a narrow passage between two huge boulders, the scene hidden from her for a few moments, but she emerged much closer and heard her breath draw in with a gasp.

A huge earthen fort, a *rath* built into the side of the mountain, jutted out. She'd seen pictures of these stone forts, some of them dating back to the Bronze Age a thousand years before Christ, almost all of them relics of pagan or early pre-Christian Celtic civilizations. Before the open doorway in front of her stood an old bearded man, a burlap-like robe around his body leaving most of his chest bare, his arms raised upward to the sky. Lighted by the huge pole that burned as it stood against the stones of the rath, he murmured in an unintelligible chant to some seven or eight figures in front of him. There were both men and women, Eileen saw, all clothed in similar burlap robes but wearing small black face masks. One girl with long, streaming black hair and a walk that slithered, moved forward to stand before the old man. Slowly she removed the top of her robe to stand bare breasted before him, swaying to and fro. The others, some on their knees, some standing, all swayed and appeared to be seized by some kind of trance. But it was the old man who held Eileen's attention. His beard and hair, brown-gray, moved gently in the night wind, and in the light of the fiery burning pole his eyes glittered like blue flame. He had a deep-etched face, fierce, cruel, hard as the cliffs of Aran and he looked as though he had stepped from an ancient century of pagan Celtic worship.

As she watched he turned, and picked up a leather-covered drum, and began to beat on it with a rhythm that gathered speed and force. The others began to dance in a loose circle led by the girl with the bare breasts and streaming black hair. As they danced and the old man drummed with one hand, he reached down with the other and lifted a stone vessel. Slowly, he poured some of the contents onto the ground. The liquid was dark red, Eileen saw, and her stomach turned over. Forcing herself not to be sick, she pressed against the rock and realized that she was observing some sort of wild cult, worshippers of the ancient, pre-Christian druidic religion. She had heard once that there were still those who tried to find their answers in the harsh, cruel barbarism of ancient rites and superstitions. It seemed to her that here in the good soil of Ireland nothing ever really died, not old hatreds, not old wounds, not old superstitions. And the latter was not so surprising for the stamp of pagan cultures, of pre-Christian Celtic life, was all over the land of the Cross. The *bullans* and *cromlechs*, *raths* and *gallans* and *tumuli* were visible reminders of the pagan past; to some, invitations more than reminders.

Eileen looked again at the stain on the ground as the old man, still drumming with one hand, put down the vessel. The pole was beginning to burn down now and the light was growing dimmer. She edged her way from the rocks and crept in a circle to skirt the scene in front of her. The dancers were stopping now, murmuring and breathing hard. She saw the bare-breasted girl walk in her sliding, slow way up to the wild-eyed, bearded man. He held out his hand and she took it, and he turned to lead her into the darkness of the stone fort. That's when Eileen's foot slipped and dislodged the half-dozen small stones. They clattered down the rocky ground. She saw the others below freeze for an instant and then turn to look up to where she was making her way around the outside of the little circle.

With an ear-splitting shout the old man pointed up to her and the others came to life. Like so many apes, they were bounding over the rocks and stones, racing toward her. Eileen turned and ran through the narrow paths of the rocks, hearing the angry shouts of the others. But it was as though she were in a maze with never-ending passages leading to unknown ends. She turned down one, then another, slipped and fell, landing hard, her hand clutching a rock. Getting up, she saw a masked figure drop down from above her to land in the narrow passageway. Murmuring angry sounds, he reached out for her. She flung the rock and saw it hit the man full in the face. He cried out in pain and staggered back, and she turned and cut down another of the defiles. She dropped into a deep shadow for an instant as she heard two others leaping across overhead, and then she ran on, glimpsing the woods beyond to the left. She pulled herself up on top of a formation of rocks and leaped across them, heading for the woods. A figure flew at her from the side and she tried to swerve, falling and rolling across the top of a flat stone. The figure flew over her, brushing against her for a moment, and then went down into one of the narrow passageways with a cry of pain. Eileen got up, and saw others coming after her across the rocks. She ran with a speed she didn't possess, plunging into the thickness of the woods, crashing against sharp branches and thorny leaves that cut into her body. They were still after her and she could hear the sound of them, behind and to the right and left of her. They were fanning out to come in on her regardless of which way she went. The ground grew steep suddenly and she felt her footing go, tried to clutch at a branch, missed, and felt the ground drop away. She fell, hitting against bits of trees and branches, bouncing off brush and jutting edges of soil. A ledge leaning out almost stopped her as she fell onto it, but then she rolled off and plunged downward again.

Still clinging to consciousness, she felt her body scream out in pain with every stab and crash on the uneven descent. Dimly she remembered being grateful that she was not falling down some steep cliff and that, for all the pain and probably smashed ribs, the obstructions were helping to break her fall. She slammed into another ledge, bounced from it, hit a tree sticking out at right angles and felt her head swimming away, a deep blackness closing down over her eyes. When she landed at the bottom she was already unconscious, unaware of the length of the mountain's long, narrow cut through which she had fallen.

When she opened her eyes, later, her pursuers still prowled the mountain side far above for her. The girl stirred, moved an arm, then the other. When she tried to sit up, she almost screamed in pain and bit her lower lip. Slowly she maneuvered herself into a sitting position. She didn't know how long she'd lain unconscious nor where she was. She only knew that she hurt all over and that she had fled from what may well have been death. Using a tree branch, she pulled herself up on her feet and began to walk, slowly, painfully, each step an excruciating experience. The ground was at least fairly level as she made her way, one slow step at a time, pausing to hold onto trees with every step, fighting down the nausea of pain. Suddenly, in front of her, she saw light on the water, pale blue but enough to reveal the lough. She hurried, gasping with the pain it brought, but keeping on, crossing the road to follow the slow circle of the shoreline. She moved along the bank, peering ahead as she did so. Colin Riorden had said his was the only cottage fronting the lough. If she kept to the bank she would reach it, if her strength held out. She paused, her legs weak, fighting down the pain. Suddenly she saw a line of figures on the road. They were moving toward her. She stayed still, watching them come closer. The darkness and distance made accurate counting impossible, but she guessed six at least, maybe more. Were they the ones who had been on the mountainside?

She couldn't be sure and she couldn't risk that they might be the same. Dropping to the moss of the bank, she crawled down it to the water, slithering into the lough on her stomach. The lough and she were becoming very well acquainted, she thought with grim irony. In the water, only the top of her head above the surface, she watched the line of people pass, more men than women, dressed in ordinary garb, and when they had gone down the road she pulled herself from the water. Shivering cold and wet, every muscle crying as her body shook, she forced herself to go on, keeping on around the edge of the water. She was beginning to despair as she felt her strength ebbing away, what little there was left of it disappearing with one wracking, shivering tremor after another. Then, as she was about to sink down onto the grass, she saw the small neat shape come into view, the flickering light of a fire inside dancing against the window. She ran forward, half-falling against the door with a loud crash. When it opened the big man stood there, frowning, and she fell into his arms as the world spiraled away once again.

CHAPTER FOUR

WARM, the wonderful, secure feeling of being warm. That was the first thing she felt when she woke, her eyes still closed. Slowly, keeping her eyes shut, she let her thoughts put themselves into place. She felt the soft wool of a blanket on her skin and knew she was naked, and finally she opened her eyes, took in the whitewashed ceiling with the oak beams crossing it, and then let her eyes roam around the small cottage. Finally they rested on the big man seated in a chair near the fireplace and behind him she saw her jeans and shirt hanging from the mantle, drying in the heat of the small fire.

"Hello," Colin Riorden said softly. "How are you feeling?"

"As though I fell down a mountainside," she replied. "Which is what I did."

"And into the lough?"

"No, I did that later, on purpose," she said.

"More strange accidents?" Colin Riorden said, the gray-blue eyes cool, probing.

"Not accidents, just horrible, terrifying things," Eileen said, shuddering under the blanket.

The big man got up and came over to the bed where she lay. He sat down at the edge of the bed and his eyes were studying her, dropping for a moment to the softly rounded whiteness of her shoulders above the edge of the blanket.

"Perhaps you'd better tell me what happened to you tonight," he said. "You certainly were in bad shape when you fell through the door. Then, when I put you into bed, you came half-awake and were murmuring something about someone chasing you."

She nodded. "Yes, I've got to tell somebody," she said. "Just promise you won't think me insane, because everything I'm going to tell you really happened. I had dinner earlier in the evening with Rory Muldoon, Lady Donegan's solicitor."

"I know," Colin Riorden said, the cool eyes steady, appraising.

"All right, so I can skip that part," Eileen said but he surprised her.

"No, please don't," he said. "Start at the beginning and tell me everything. I always like hearing what other people have to say and think. It's the historian in me, I guess, and Muldoon's a professional man, a knowledgeable fellow."

Eileen shrugged and quickly told him of her dinner and what Rory had said about the tensions and troubles in the land. Colin Riorden listened, his eyes narrowed, his intentness a physical, tangible thing as he absorbed her every word as though he were recording it in his mind. Every once in a while he'd have her repeat something Rory had said, a sentence, a piece of the philosophical talk they'd had on the nature of evil. But finally she finished with Rory's part of the evening, skipping the kiss outside the door of the great house, though, feeling strangely malicious, she toyed with the idea of throwing that in, too.

"Are things really that troubled, Colin?" she asked the quiet man.

"They're troubled," he said. "In all kinds of ways."

She went on to tell him how she'd gone to her room, undressed, and lay musing on the bed when she heard the sound of the fife. She admitted it had been a foolish thing to go chasing into the night after it, and, though he said nothing, she had the distinct feeling he agreed with her. She went on to losing the sound of the fife and then herself on the mountain and stumbling onto the wild and weird ceremony of druidic worship. When she finished her story she felt her body trembling again under the blanket.

"There was something terrifying about it," she said. "It wasn't just uncivilized, pagan. It was depraved, animalistic, hypnotic, full of strange symbolism."

She thought of the huge pole being consumed instead of an ordinary fire, and she began to see the phallic symbolism and the sexual emphasis in other bits and pieces she had been too astonished to really note at the time.

"The old man," Colin said, musing aloud, his gray-blue eyes grave. "The old *mullagh* man."

"The old what?" Eileen asked.

"That's what he's known as," Colin said. "The old mullagh man, the old man of the summit. He's lived up there in the rath for more years than people can remember, I'm told. But I'd wager there are dammed few who know he practices druidic sacrificial ceremonies. There'd be the devil to pay about that."

"Why?"

"Druidic sacrificial worship is against the law," Colin said. "It's banned, outlawed, and the penalties for the practice of it are severe. It leads to the kind of excesses you can well guess at on your own."

"I was afraid they were going to kill me if they caught me," Eileen said. "I could sense it by the way they came after me, like so many animals."

"You could have been right about that," he said. "And none of the others were recognizable at all."

"No, they all wore masks," she said. Though, inwardly, she felt she could recognize the bare-breasted girl by her walk. But it was only a thought and she didn't voice it. Colin Riorden was studying her again, his cool eyes watching her intently.

"And so after you fell, and hid in the lake from the people that came by, you found your way here," he said.

Eileen nodded. "I remembered what you said about your cottage fronting the lake," she said.

"I'm glad of that," he said. "And I'm glad you found your way here. But I want to warn you not to tell this story to others. Right now you have no proof and, though I certainly believe you, other people might not. There's no way of knowing who is involved in this sacrificial druidic cult with the old mullagh man. Probably not many, but one is enough to be dangerous. You've had enough strange troubles without adding those of a warped, demented person to them."

"You mean someone who might be afraid if I talked about what I'd seen and try to silence me," she said.

"Something like that," he said. "I promise to bring this to the attention of the proper authorities in time."

"Meanwhile, it'll certainly add to your historical research," she said, and he smiled and nodded. "You're right, of course," she said. "Good God, I've enough talent for getting into trouble without adding more."

Suddenly the scene on the mountainside was in front of her eyes again and she was trembling. She felt a large, steady hand on her shoulder.

"There, now, take it slow," he said. "You'll sleep here the rest of the night." He looked down at her and his eyes almost twinkled in the flickering light of the fire.

"Unless you'd rather go back to Drumroe," he said.

She met his eyes and knew he was reading her thoughts. His cabin was snug and warm and so much more appealing than the thought of returning to the severe, forbidding vastness of the huge house.

"No, I'd much rather stay here," she said. The slow, Cheshire-cat smile that crossed his face was too self-satisfied to just let go. "I imagine I've about run through my quota of close calls for one night," she said and had the satisfaction of seeing him turn to study her again.

"I expect so," he agreed quietly. "But before you go to sleep I'll make you a good pot of hot tea. You're in need of that."

Eileen rose on one elbow. "Could I have coffee, please?" she asked.

"Ah, the American in you coming through," he said. "Sorry, but it'll have to be tea."

"Tea it is," she said, sinking back and hearing the pout in her voice. "I don't mean to sound ungrateful," she added, "but doesn't anyone ever drink coffee in this whole country?" She heard his soft chuckle.

"There are some philistines," he said. "And I'm sure we can find some coffee for you somewhere this side of Belfast or Dublin."

He had put the big kettle on the fire, and now he put a wooden stool beside the bed where she could drink and still remain fairly modest. He set two cups on the stool, brought the kettle over, and poured the hot water into a small china teapot. Letting it steep awhile, he finally poured the tea. Taking his cup, he moved back to sit comfortably at the foot of the bed, sipping from the steaming cup of tea with relish. She half-rose, not really caring that the blanket revealed a good part of the beauty of her firm, young breasts. Somehow, it seemed not at all wrong with this quiet, cool-eyed man. She smiled at the way he savored the hot tea.

"Now, if I have to drink coffee, I'd prefer to do it the way the French used to in the Ardennes," he said. "I hear they still drink it that way. It's a custom there to take ten small cups of coffee after dinner."

"Ten?" she echoed.

"Ten," he nodded gravely. "And each cup has its own special name. The first one is *Café*, with milk in it. The second is called *Gloria*, the third *Pousse Café*, then *Goutte, Regoutte, Surgoutte, Rincette, Re-rincette, Sur-rincette* and number ten, *Coup de l'étrier*. The *Gloria* had a small glass of brandy in place of the milk and every cup after it had a little greater amount of brandy until the last one, the *Coup de l'étrier,* which we call the stirrup cup. Now that, my girl, is the only way to drink coffee."

Eileen laughed, a feat she would have thought impossible a little while ago. "You know, I was going to come see you anyway, tomorrow," she said. "I'm terribly worried about my aunt. It's just not like her to send for me and then take off without any word. You spoke to her last week, you told me. Did she say anything you can remember about going away, a name or a place, anything at all?"

She saw the line of his jaw harden as he shook his head.

"She didn't use her cars nor did she use O'Leary's Livery Service," Eileen said.

When Colin's eyes turned to her, they were a hard gray, boring through her. "Been doing a little one-girl investigating, I see," he remarked. There was no smile in his voice, either. She recalled the astonishment on his face when she'd introduced herself at the lough yesterday morning. There was a subtle hint of danger to this man, that held-back feeling she'd sensed before. Then why did she feel attracted to him, comfortable in his presence? Was she fated to be attracted to the unknown, to the night, to the smell of danger, she wondered. The relaxing warmth of the tea had curled itself around her and she suddenly felt very sleepy, too sleepy to stay awake. She felt her eyes close, saw a brief glimpse of Colin sitting down in the chair by the fire, and then she was asleep, breathing deeply, her head a circle of dark flame on the pillow.

She slept not soundly but hard, unconscious of the way her hands quivered from time to time or the way in which her lovely face turned from side to side. In the depths of her sleep she saw not the most immediate terrors, not the old mullagh man, not his druidic ceremony, but strangely disjointed images that went far back into the past. She saw her wedding night with Chuck, the morning of her mother's funeral, and she saw herself whirling inside a black funnel, spinning around helplessly, controlled by something beyond her own self. Suddenly she saw Colin Riorden's face and felt her nakedness under the wool blanket, and it seemed very natural to be naked before his gray-blue eyes. The images switched off abruptly and she lay in solid darkness, an uneasy darkness that lasted for more time than she knew. The fire burned out in the cabin and it was the waiting hour between the dark and the dawn. That was the moment she was seized by the terrible coldness twisting inside her, demanding, refusing to be put aside. She flung herself from side to side of the little bed, possessed by other voices from other places, sounds and sights and searing things that burned with a cold fire. Suddenly she sat bolt upright, her dark blue eyes snapping open, but only dimly aware of the big man hurriedly getting up from the chair, not caring that the blanket had fallen to her waist as she sat up. Only one thought possessed her, one screaming, terrible thought.

"Aunt Agnes is dead!" she screamed out the phrase. "She's dead, dead!"

Then, as though she had suddenly been released from a terrible bondage, her breath gasped out in a deep rush of air, and she sank back, quivering, pulling the blanket up before her. Colin was beside her now and she reached out and pulled herself against him, clinging to him as she trembled, not oblivious of her breasts pressing into his chest, but just not caring. It felt good to be held. The terrible cold flame was still inside her, though not burning with the same intensity.

"A nightmare, Eileen," she heard him say. "There, now, just relax."

"No, no nightmare," she said into his chest. "I know! God, I know. It's something that happens to me, a vision, a premonition, call it whatever you like, but I know."

Colin stepped back, and she pulled the blanket around her. His eyes were probing into her intently.

"You've had things like this before?" he asked. She nodded, feeling the tears well in her eyes.

"Yes, and they've always been right," she half-sobbed. "I've had a terrible dread inside me for days now. I thought maybe it was a premonition of what happened to me at the lough. But now I know that wasn't it. Now I know what it was."

She saw his eyes watching her. "She's dead," Eileen said. "I just saw her dead. You can be certain of it."

Quickly, the girl told Colin of the other times, or of most of them, starting with that first night when she was but twenty. When she finished her eyes were deep and staring, looking at him for an understanding she knew she could not have, an understanding no one could really give her.

"I feel, sometimes, as though I'm one of the damned, one of the possessed, given powers to torture me," she said. "I don't want this cursed thing. I don't want to see these things. Ever since it first happened I've lived in a private kind of hell, never knowing when I'm getting some kind of special communication until suddenly I'm possessed by something I can't control. And I can't control it. God, I've tried that, but it doesn't work. I've tried to foresee things, to concentrate on someone and know what they're doing. But nothing happens then. It comes to me in its own way and in its own time. It's like being owned by something or someone you can't see or know or yell at."

She felt her sobs coming and they exploded inside her as her words had exploded in the little cottage. It had taken all these years to talk to someone about it and now, here, it had all come out, a tower of fear that had to collapse.

"Why does it terrify you so?" Colin asked. "Because you feel helpless before it?"

"Helpless and as though I've never really known myself," Eileen said. "It's as though I've never been free of other voices, other influences."

"Are you so terrified of it because you can't forget that an ancestor of yours was burned as a witch here in 1790?" he asked quietly.

"How did you know about that?"

"I'm an historian, remember?" he said. "I've been digging into the history of the House of Drumroe. How much has that bit of ancient history bothered you, honestly, now?"

"Not much," Eileen said, and immediately knew she wasn't certain of her answer. "At least, I don't think so," she corrected herself. "I've thought about it some, I admit. But I don't believe in things like witches and stupid old superstitions."

"But you believe in premonitions, in visions," he said.

"I have to believe in them," Eileen answered. "They've all been so terribly right."

"Then believe in them, but don't let them terrify you," Colin Riorden said as she sat back. "Clairvoyances, extrasensory perceptions, premonitions, all those things are accepted as existing. We don't know enough about them, about how and why they operate, but we're sure they do operate. Not for everybody, of course, though we all may have some mild ability in that area. The powers of clairvoyance have been described as working a bit like radio signals. We're all receiving sets, getting chemical, biological, and electrical signals from each other and from all kinds of sources. You could say that most of us are such weak receivers that we pick up very little. However, a few people are like extrapowerful receiving stations, and they pick up all kinds of signals denied to the rest of us. Those are the clairvoyant, the extrasensory perceptors."

"Me," Eileen grunted, and Colin nodded. "You make it sound so reasonable with that explanation," she said.

"It's an analogy not an explanation," he corrected. "And it means that we know so little that all we can do is to draw very rational, oversimplified analogies. The truth is that the areas of psychic transmission are so shrouded in the unknown that we have damn little idea of how to scientifically approach learning about them. In fact, maybe the usual scientific methods will have to be discarded in exploring the whole subject of psychic phenomena."

Eileen's thoughts had again keyed into what Rory Muldoon had said about the transmission of evil, of a disease of the mind, and she shuddered. Colin's reasonable analogy was suddenly much less reassuring. She looked up at him with grave eyes.

"It isn't all that important," she lied. "What matters is that Aunt Agnes is dead."

His eyes were gray stone again, and she saw the line of his jaw grow rigid.

"You're convinced of it," he said. "Perhaps your little vision gave you some details such as where, when or how."

She saw his eyes on her and she shook her head, almost with a sense of shame at having failed at the important things.

"I told you all it does is possess you," she answered. "It only calls out what it wants to say and never anything more. And it makes you do things you wouldn't do otherwise, just to prove you are your own master. Of course, they don't work and all you've proven is that you're a damn fool."

"How did you prove that?" Colin asked.

"By getting married," Eileen answered, bitterness filling her voice, surprising her by its presence.

"Want to talk about it?" Colin asked. Eileen eyed the big man's serious face with a frown. She had never spoken of her marriage to anyone, except in a surface kind of way, but now she wanted very much to tell about it. It leaped forward, insistent, demanding to be looked at again out loud, and she wondered if this weren't part of the price for finding herself. And so, in the stillness of the daybreak hour, she heard her voice telling about her marriage, the images coming back to her with unvarnished candor. It was a sense of unburdening that seized her, and she began at that party where she had first met Chuck. Her mother had been dead some eight months and she had taken her own new apartment. She told of the searching days, and how she still clung to the fear of her beauty betraying herself or someone else. It was almost funny, as she thought back on it, how not betraying

Chuck had been so in the forefront of her mind. She had come to know how easily she could captivate men, how the burnished copper of her hair and her soft, sensuous body could enthrall. But Chuck, Charles Edgar Hopkins, had been different from the others. Handsome, charming, and wealthy, he had been many places and seen beauty in many forms. He was definitely not the type to need protecting. Still, she was careful at first, wanting to be sure, for him more than for herself. To her, Chuck Hopkins seemed the end of searching, the wonderful man every girl hopes to meet and marry. When he asked her to marry him, all her doubts and cautions had long since vanished. He had assured her he loved her for herself. And she, of course, loved him, with the kind of desperate love only those running from themselves can give. Chuck's parents insisted on a large wedding, though she would have preferred something simple with Father Ryan from St. Joseph's. Chuck's father knew the cardinal, though, and so the wedding became a big thing with lots of gay, ebullient friends and acquaintances. The wedding night, alone with Chuck in a cottage in the Bahamas, was made for glory and ecstasy and all the things a girl should remember forever and ever. She remembered, all right, her silent cry that would echo inside her from that moment.

"Make love to me, Chuck, make love to me," she had whispered to him, and he had turned her body into a leaping pillar of ecstasy. He knew how to play her body, and when she reached that explosion of the flesh she realized a terrible thing. Where there should have been a consuming fulfillment, there was a blinding flash of emptiness. He was there, his body hard against hers, but she heard a terrible voice inside her cry out: "But where are *you*, Chuck, where are *you*?"

When he finished, she was ashamed for her unnerving thoughts, for the fact that she had felt so much physical pleasure made her silent question seem not only ungrateful, but altogether improper. She thrust it aside, marking it down as one of those strange reactions that people sometimes have at moments of extreme emotion. She refused to even think anything else. Chuck was the end of searching, the perfect man, and she wouldn't let anything interfere with her happiness. Least of all nasty hidden messages from some inner voice.

Chuck worked for his father's firm of Wall Street lawyers, but they decided to live in her modest apartment. Chuck seemed to enjoy playing the role of struggling young newlyweds, though they attended parties and went out on a scale no struggling young marrieds could ever afford. And when each day came to an end and she was in bed in his arms, he would make love to her with that expertness that brought her screaming to a pitch of physical ecstasy. She didn't want to scream, at first, but then it covered the insistent inner voice that kept crying out for something more. More? she asked herself as she lay beside his sleeping form afterward. More what? Certainly not more physical pleasure. Was there something wrong with her, she wondered. Did she want more than there was? Again, she refused to let her inner misgivings destroy her happiness. But they were there, inside her, and though she could refuse to heed them, she could not ignore them. So she plunged herself fully into everything that she could do to make Chuck happy. She went with him to every cocktail party he wanted to attend, though they became a bore after a while. She let him show his beautiful wife off at important business meetings, sometimes only putting in a brief appearance at the right moment, just as he wanted it done. And always, in the deep of the night, she whispered, "Make love to me, Chuck." And he would make love to her, playing her body with an experienced skill that was not to be denied, and she certainly wasn't about to deny it. His ability to bring her to heights of physical pleasure had become almost a craving for her, a terrible need, and she refused to wonder why.

They'd been married for over six months when Sam and Sarah Grossman invited them to a party. Chuck wanted to back out, but Eileen had insisted and so he'd gone along. It was the first time she'd ever seen her charming, debonair, witty Chuck be a sullen bore. He obviously cared nothing about anyone there and, while he had always been his usual charming self to Sam and Sarah during brief neighborly meetings, this time he was barely polite. Eileen made excuses about not feeling well and they left early, a dark shame and hurt inside her. In the solitude of their apartment, she spoke to Chuck, more in wonder than in anger.

"Why?" she asked, wishing she didn't sound so damned plaintive. "Why were you so obviously bored and unfriendly? They were all perfectly nice people."

"They were a lot of perfectly nothing," he said coldly. "There wasn't one person there I could give a damn about."

"You mean there wasn't anyone there you felt worth impressing," Eileen said, her dark blue eyes looking at him with a warning in them he failed to read.

"Put it that way if you like," he answered.

"Impressing people is what it's all about with you, isn't it, Chuck?" Eileen said. "Is that why you married me, to impress people with a beautiful wife?"

He hesitated a moment and then gave her one of the special Chuck Hopkins grins, the kind, she suddenly saw, that impressed you with how charming he was.

"That's pretty silly stuff," he said. "I married you because I love you. I'll prove it to you again right now."

He grabbed her, flung her on the bed roughly, and proceeded to make love to her in his expert way and, despite herself, she felt her body responding to his every touch, his every movement. But it was as though she were two people, one of them responding with fevered desire, the other hanging back, searching, waiting for something that wasn't there. When her scream of ecstasy came, as it always did under his skillful hands and he lay atop her, holding her tight, he whispered in her ear. "How about that?" he said. "Proof enough?"

How about that, she repeated silently to herself. The expert lover is pressed against me but where are you, Chuck, she asked silently. Where are you? He rolled to one side and in seconds she heard the steady sound of his breathing as he fell asleep. It hadn't been proof enough, not of what she wanted. It took her a long time to sleep, almost till dawn, and she was still asleep when he left in the morning. That night he called to say he'd be out late with a client.

Work seemed to pile up for the firm and Chuck began staying out late at least two or three nights a week. He would come home too tired to do anything but fall into bed those nights but in between, at the other times when they were together, he made love to her with an efficiency that seemed almost automatic. She kept telling herself it was all her own wild thinking. She even put aside that time at Sam and Sarah's party. If impressing people was important to Chuck, if he needed to be around people he wanted to impress, then that was his own little idiosyncrasy.

She would understand. She was becoming very good at making excuses for Chuck, for herself, for all the persistent, nagging questions. Her craving to hide in the obliterating release of his lovemaking grew worse. She refused to realize that the desperation was in direct ratio to the persistence of the questions.

The party at Cynthia Dennison's apartment added suspicions to questions. Cynthia worked at the law firm, too, as a legal secretary, and it was the usual cocktail party with Chuck being his warm, witty, charming self. He made sure to introduce Eileen to two new and important clients, both of whom frankly admired her beauty. She enjoyed their admiration. It was later, when a slight headache took her into the bathroom on a search for aspirin, that she heard Cynthia and a girl named Barbara something-or-other in the adjoining bedroom.

"When is Chuck going to move out of the horrid little apartment and come into the neighborhood?" Barbara was asking.

"Not for a while, I'd say," Cynthia answered. "That horrid little apartment keeps his little Eileen tucked out of the way. If they lived here she'd be too apt to bump into Chuck and the current girl-of-the-month."

"Who is current with dear Chuck?" Eileen heard the other girl ask. Cynthia's laugh held a slight maliciousness.

"Ask Chuck, dear," she said. "Or get in line."

Eileen waited until she heard them go back to the party and then she slipped out to rejoin the others. She was really astonished at herself. She felt no fury, no seething anger. She didn't even feel particularly wronged and wondered why. She insisted Chuck take her home early, using the headache as an excuse. She wanted to return to her apartment and to think, to ask herself questions and face the answers once and for all. But mostly, at that moment, she wondered why she wasn't more seething, more the furious, wronged wife.

When they returned home that night, Chuck lay beside her, his hands, his lips, running over her body, turning on the desire he knew was waiting there. She let him make love to her, but this time she was not merely two people with one hanging back. This time a part of her was a spectator as, with a sense of admiration for Chuck, she felt her body respond to his expertness. Finally, at that moment of moments, one question at least became an answer. She even understood why it had flown through her mind on their wedding night.

During the next few days she idly speculated on which of the many girls she'd met at the many cocktail parties was Chuck's current girl-of-the-month, as Cynthia had phrased it. It wasn't even a vengeful speculation or a heart-breaking wonder. She was more curious than anything else. It was almost funny how once she had been so concerned about her beauty betraying Chuck, when all the while she had been the one betrayed. It was at the end of the week, Friday, that Chuck called to say he'd be out very late with a client, entertaining new contacts. She said something appropriate, ate alone, watched television, and finally went to bed. A hard, rocklike core of bitterness had filled her, but there was still no anger, no fury, and at last she understood why. It was because she had known from their wedding night, known without consciously knowing, and now what was coming clear gave her a sense of confirmation, bitter confirmation. Anger had been used up, bit by bit, ironically, with every moment of ecstasy in Chuck's hands. She went to sleep, a fitful, tossing sleep that ended as suddenly as it had began. She woke up and saw Chuck with Cora Neilson, one of the girls she'd had on her mental list, a small, pert dress model. Eileen found the girl's address in the phone book, dressed, and went to her apartment. It was two o'clock in the morning, and she had the taxi wait downstairs. She was only going there to put a final stamp of defeat on something lost long ago. Chuck was just coming out of Cora Neilson's apartment, the girl's naked body still pressed to him in a goodnight embrace. Eileen halted, met Chuck's astonished eyes, and simply turned and hurried back to the waiting taxi.

Chuck got to their place a few minutes after she had arrived, and the uncertainty of his eyes told her he didn't know what to expect. Her cool, bitter calmness was beyond him and somewhat unnerving, she was pleased to note.

"Let's not make a big thing out of this, Eileen," he began. "I can explain about Cora."

"I'm sure you can, Chuck," she answered. "Cora is really unimportant. But you aren't. She was only a symptom. You're the trouble."

"What does that mean?" he asked, frowning suspiciously.

"It means I understand now what I felt a long time ago," Eileen said simply. "It means I know what I knew that first night we were married. I just refused to listen to myself then or even believe it. I remember how you were with me that night, Chuck, and how you've been every night since then in bed. You were so expert, so wonderful, and that's who was in bed with me, Chuck

Hopkins, the expert lover. Chuck Hopkins, a man in love, wasn't there. He wasn't there because he doesn't exist. Only Chuck Hopkins, the expert lover, exists. You make love, Chuck, you don't love. In one way or another people are things for you to impress. That's how you get your kicks, impressing others, every one in a different way."

"Why'd I marry you, then?" he blurted out. "Why didn't I just impress you with my abilities without marrying you."

Eileen's full, red lips were tinged with a sad smile as she replied. "That wouldn't have impressed me, if I'd have let you," she said. "And then you needed a wife, a beautiful wife to impress others on your way up the business ladder of success. So I was it. Oh, it was my fault, too, that part of getting married. I was searching, trying desperately to find happiness like everyone else. I took a wrong turn. You."

"We've been happy, Eileen," Chuck said, putting his hands on her shoulders. They were fingers of ice that did nothing but chill her. "I sure as hell made you happy in bed, and that's plenty for most women."

"No, you didn't make me happy. You made me physically satisfied, gloriously and completely satisfied. But even that first time I felt there was something missing, that something called caring, loving, feeling with something more than your body. We've been bodies twisted around each other, a kind of fervency of the flesh, and nothing more. It's the height of irony, I guess, but I know now that every time you made love to me, our relationship got a little emptier. Everytime you made my body throb with that singular kind of desire, it made what was missing that much more clear. I just wouldn't let myself face the truth."

"And now you're going to play the wronged wife?" he said, using sarcasm for defense.

"No, I'm just going to divorce you," Eileen said simply. "It's funny but I don't really feel wronged. You wronged the meaning of love more than you did me. You wrong the meaning of everything you do, Chuck. You wrong the spirit of charm, the fun of wit, the meaning of sex. You wrong everything because none of it is real with you. Everything is a tool, a device to impress someone else. You don't like people, Chuck. You only like impressing those you think worth trying to impress. It's a sort of victory each time for you, a small battle you win. When there's no one you think worth winning over, as that time at Sam and Sarah's party, you're not interested."

"What if I said I don't understand any of this stuff you're sounding off about?" he demanded. "What if I said I didn't believe it and I thought you were just having a nice case of quiet hysterics."

Eileen smiled at her charming, debonair, handsome, empty husband, a rueful slow smile. "I'd believe you," she replied. "I'm sure you don't understand because you can't."

"How did you know I was with Cora Neilson tonight?" he asked, watching her intently. "How'd you find out?"

"I just knew," she said wearily. "And you wouldn't understand that, either." She turned away, feeling very drained and saddened all of a sudden.

"Good-bye, Chuck," she said. "Believe me, there's nothing more to say."

Chuck got some things and walked out. He was probably going back to Cora Neilson's, and she didn't really care. She was too filled with bitterness at herself to care, and as the days grew into weeks and months, the bitterness only crystallized into a leaden weight that hung around her. She began divorce proceedings, despite those who felt she had to live with her mistakes, and time let her become a stable, hard-working, pleasant girl again. She learned to live with her own bitterness, and she came to know, over many long walks and long nights, the meaning of the line in Aunt Agnes's letter about looking for happiness in the wrong places. She had tried to find happiness and thought it could make her find herself when, she knew now, you have to find yourself before you can find happiness.

That was only a few short weeks before the last letter came from Aunt Agnes asking her to hurry to Drumroe. And now, thoroughly exhausted by reliving her marriage again in her memory, she looked up at the big, quiet man sitting on the edge of the bed.

"So you see, even there, other voices from other places told me things. I didn't listen and I was sorry, sorry and wrong," she said.

"And you're convinced Lady Donegan is dead," Colin Riorden said. She nodded her head gravely. The morning light was flooding into the little cottage and he stood up.

"I don't agree with you," he said.

"But you sounded as though you did believe in clairvoyance, in extrasensory powers," Eileen protested.

"I said I believed in the existence of such phenomena," Colin answered quickly. "I don't think you experienced such a thing this time, not a correct one, at least. I'd say your state of worry over your aunt brought about your nightmare."

She wanted to say she'd never been wrong before, but she held her tongue. There had been visions in the night which hadn't seemed to mean anything, but she knew that was because she misinterpreted them or couldn't make the explanatory connection. Yet she couldn't rationally explain this to Colin, or to anyone.

"Why don't you believe me?" she asked instead.

"Let's say I'm a practical man," Colin answered. "Lady Donegan was alive and here a few days ago. We've plenty of witnesses to that. She went away the day before you were to arrive, so far as we can tell. Cladvale and this countryside isn't all that big, my girl. If she'd had an accident, her body would have been discovered by now. Even if she'd gone to the shore cliffs and fallen over, the sea washes in its victims, and there are always fishermen and shore walkers mucking about someplace."

"What if she met with something other than an accident?" Eileen asked levelly. Colin's glance was quick, sharp, piercing.

"Now what makes you think a thing like that, girl?" he asked. "Because of that strange accident of yours by the lough?"

"Maybe. I don't really know," Eileen said. "But I thought it and that's what counts."

"You're talking about murder and that's a nasty word, to say the least," Colin answered slowly. "First, there's got to be a motive. But let's assume someone had a motive. Murder isn't all that easy. First, when you murder someone, you've got to dispose of the body."

"Well, there are certainly woods enough around here to do that," Eileen shot back. He seemed to be searching for reasons why she had to be wrong.

"True, there are woods enough, and it might seem a simple thing in the telling," Colin said. "But in the doing, it doesn't usually work out that way. You can't just dig a hole anywhere. First you've got to hide the body, and then carry it to wherever you want to dispose of it. That all takes time and cunning and planning and a good bit of luck, too."

"How do you know so much about it?" Eileen asked, sounding sharper than she had intended to sound. He smiled back at her. "I'm a detective story fan when I'm not being an historian," he said.

He turned and went to the door. "No, I'll just not buy your flash of vision, Eileen," he said. "I'll go outside for a moment while you put on your things. They'll be dry by now."

Eileen watched him close the door, and she swung from the bed and hurried to where her jeans and shirt hung, a long, lovely, cream white figure in the morning light. She didn't agree with Colin Riorden's practical approach. She thought of the fog-bound nights and knew that they could be a cloak for anything. Her clothes on her, warm from the fire, she went out to where Colin stood gazing across the misted surface of the lough. She felt very small beside him, strange, afraid and yet secure, attracted to this man whose eyes held more than they revealed. They were very different, these two men she had met here, Rory Muldoon with his rakish, taut charm, and Colin with his restrained quietness. But, then, this land was a land of contrasts. Rory was certainly not the typical lawyer, and Colin far from the typical historian.

She touched his sleeve lightly, tentatively. "Colin, if you don't believe in what I saw in my dream or whatever you want to call it, what do you think has happened to Lady Donegan?"

His eyes stayed narrowed and there was a hardness in them as he looked down at her. "I'm sure she hasn't left here by any of the usual roads or methods," he said. "Perhaps she has closeted herself somewhere not far away to see how people, including you, will react to her absence."

Eileen turned the thought over in her mind and wondered briefly what made him so certain Aunt Agnes hadn't left the community. But his thought was not without possibilities. She watched him for another moment, trying unsuccessfully to read behind those eyes. He was a strange man, this Colin Riorden, but a compelling one. And she owed him something more than a simple thank-you for his understanding and help.

"Molly McConnell promised to cook a good dinner for me tonight," she said. "She'd be even happier if I had someone else to enjoy it. Will you come? Seven o'clock?"

"A good meal is something never to be turned down," he answered. "It will be my pleasure."

She left him there beside the cottage and went down the road in the early day, dark copper hair picking up the first glinting of the new sun. All the things that had happened to her in the night lay heavy on her, but the heaviest was her vision of death. She would call Rory and get his reactions to it and to what had happened to her. The big awesomeness of the towering house of

Drumroe rose up in front of her, standing like the strange enigmatic thing it was, harboring echoes from the past that were more than echoes. She hurried forward just as Brannock came out the front door, his eyes mirroring his surprise at seeing her.

"I decided on an early walk this morning," she lied smoothly. "Is Molly about? I'm hungry."

He nodded and his gaunt, deep-eyed face turned away, the silent hostility of the man unmistakable. She went inside and heard Molly in the kitchen. She had lied to Brannock about the early walk but not about being hungry. Besides, she wanted to tell Molly they'd be having an extra guest for dinner.

CHAPTER FIVE

MOLLY HAD served her a large plate of *rashers* with good Irish soda bread and quince jelly, and she had sat down in the kitchen to eat, glad for the cook's stout, cheerful presence.

"It's strange not hearing from Lady Donegan by now," Molly admitted, her round face clouded. "But if she'd had an accident, I'm sure we'd have heard by now."

Eileen grunted silently. A little of Colin Riorden's theory, that was. "No news is good news, they say," Molly added.

"I've asked someone in for dinner tonight, Molly," Eileen said. "Colin Riorden. He lives in that cottage down by the lough."

"Him is it?" Molly said, brightening. "He's an odd sort in a way."

"How do you mean?"

"He does an awful lot of walking and looking about," Molly replied. "I keep meeting him all over the place. Lady Donegan remarked that she did, too."

Eileen tabled the comment. "Part of being an historian, I guess, Molly," she answered, but inside herself she wondered how true that glib reply really was.

"Well, part of being a good cook is having fresh vegetables, and that's why I've my own little garden out back," Molly went on. "Mulligan, the fish man, will be by today. I'll get a nice fresh salmon and make you poached salmon with Erin sauce."

"Sounds wonderful," Eileen said.

"Meanwhile, I'll go out back and get some fresh parsley and some carrots and some of my own good praties. Boiled and buttered, they're wonderful with salmon," Molly said.

"I'll come help," Eileen said, glancing at the clock on the wall. It was still early to call Rory at the office number he had given her. She followed the little woman's round, solid form out into the rear of the huge house. The small well-tended garden stretched back from the house. On the left she saw the good-sized bed of praties, the stems and vines easily visible. Her eyes traveled up past the garden to the small hillside beyond and to the right where the gravestones rested, the small cemetery she had seen earlier.

"The cemetery on the hill, Molly, is that the Donegan family plot?" Eileen asked. "The traditional cemetery of the House of Drumroe?"

"Indeed it is," Molly said. "Though mostly it holds those who've died here on this soil or someplace in Ireland. There's a lot who'd passed on in other lands that aren't there. Would you like a closer look?"

Eileen nodded and was grateful for the older woman's unspoken understanding of her curiosity as they walked up the side of the gentle hill.

"Lady Donegan's headstone is there in place," Molly said. "She had it put down a few years ago. She's a grand lady, she is. She's even given me permission to rest there with the family if I'd like."

"You've been with her a long time, Molly?"

"A long time it is," the cook said, both pride and pensiveness in her voice.

"Have you noticed anything worrying her lately, anything that could explain her sudden... *disappearance*?" Eileen felt her voice catch on the last word. Aunt Agnes's letter had spoken of her anxiety and the girl wondered if the older woman had been told of it, too.

"Not in so many words," Molly replied thoughtfully. "I know she's spent a lot of time in the library with the family scrapbook and newspaper clippings of late. But that could just be an old woman pleasuring herself in memories."

They had reached the top of the hill and the small graveyard, and Eileen's eyes flickered over the old headstones. There were names she recognized from family talk and a good many she didn't. Each headstone was an echo of another distant time and when she paused before one—small, weathered, chipped—she had to stop herself from trembling as a cold wind whirled through her body. MONICA DONEGAN -1790. That was all the inscription the small stone carried. Turning away quickly, she hurried on and found herself before the newest stone, gray marble and still shiny. She read the unfinished inscription:

Lady Agnes Donegan of Drumroe 1899 -

A neat square of green grass fronted the headstone, and in the center of it was a large bed of violets, a blue square tightly packed with the small delicately blue flowers and their deep green leaves. Those in the foreground of the blue square looked up at her and drank in the morning sun that beamed down. She found herself staring at the wild flowers and felt the frown creasing her brow. Why, she asked herself silently. Why did she frown? Something had disturbed her, made her frown, but whatever it was lay hidden in the dim recesses of her mind, unwilling to reveal itself. Perhaps, she told herself, it had merely been the thought of Aunt Agnes again. But even as she turned away she knew that wasn't it. There'd been something else, something that had not yet formed a thought. She cast a glance back at the square of blue-violet flowers fringed with the bright green of the grass. It was a lovely sight and she wondered why it had made her frown, a frown that stayed inside her now, one more thing among the unanswered questions there. She turned to the cook. "Thanks for coming up with me, Molly," Eileen said gratefully. "I'm not much for cemeteries."

"Neither is your aunt, but she's a practical woman," Molly said. "Better to be prepared at all times, she often said to me. She knows people, too. She finds out about them in her own ways. I remember—good Lord it's a long time now—when I first came to work for her. Whenever anything troublesome came up, a fight with the meat man or the fish peddler, she'd be unavailable, and I'd have to handle it myself. It was her way of proving me out."

Eileen glanced down at Molly, but the little woman was trudging along beside her consumed in her own memories. Yet, her words brought what Colin had said leaping to the fore. Perhaps she had been too hasty in dismissing his thought. Yet, despairingly, she knew she could not turn aside the vision in the night. Others could scoff and be skeptical, but not she. It was the gift of the damned, perhaps, but one she had to listen to. It wasn't a question of believing. It was simply a matter of knowing. Yet now the knowing was so horrible that she clutched at every rational, reasonable thing that could give her hope. Just as she had done during those years with Chuck, she recalled grimly. There was always the chance that this time her premonitions had gone wrong. It was there, a straw to cling to in hope. It was ironic, she mused silently. Most people went around hoping their insights were right while she ached for hers to be wrong.

They had reached the house and the garden, and Eileen took in the parsley, carrots, and onions while Molly stayed to dig up some praties. Inside, after putting the vegetables on the kitchen table, she hurried to the phone in the library and called Rory.

"Will you be at your office for a while?" she asked. "There are some things I want to tell you about. Last night was quite a night."

"I'll be here," he said. "My curiosity wouldn't let me leave." She heard the chuckle in his voice, and the easy self-assurance that was his made her feel better at once. "I'll be down soon," she said and hung up. Thanking drip-dry fabrics, she changed into a pair of deep orange slacks and a white blouse, and hurried out of the house. She saw Brannock sawing some logs near the garage and, looking back past the house as she headed up the road for Cladvale, her eyes swept past the little cemetery. The small frown passed across her face again as she wondered what had bothered her about the headstone. Turning away, she hurried on, and in only a few minutes Cladvale, toylike in the sun, was before her. She remembered Colin's admonishment to tell no one of last night. But, of course, that wouldn't include Rory. He was hardly one of the townspeople. As she walked down the main street, she saw even fewer people than she had before. Two old men looked at her with dark frowns, their faces cold and set, and Eileen wondered why she drew such stares. A younger man with a basket of chickens was no friendlier in his glance. The modest steeple of the church was nearly in front of her when she found herself in the middle of the village market square. There was a good sprinkling of tradesmen's and flower vendor's bright carts, some blue with orange wheels and shafts. Most of them were unattended. A crowd was gathered around a speaker only some twenty yards from the steps of the church, and Eileen moved to the edge to hear his words. He was young, black haired with blazing blue eyes, had the strong, thick hands of a farmer and the voice of an evangelist.

"It's time to rise up again," he shouted to the crowd. "The trouble has never gone away. It's always been there; a dagger pointed at the heart of free Ireland and now they've begun to stab with it again. But this time we'll finish what the patriots started that Easter morning. Till the land runs red, we'll fight. There'll be no agreements, no compromises this time."

Eileen listened to cheers from the others and suddenly she was conscious of a woman staring at her. "You're the Lady Donegan's niece from America," the woman said, her voice hard. "Come to help the old lady stand above us all again?"

"Maybe she's come to take over," another woman snapped. "The Donegan's have always been apart from everybody, whether they're witchin' or weaselin'."

"I don't know what you're talking about," Eileen said, seeing all faces turned to her. She could feel the temper of the crowd, hostile and angry.

"Don't tell us you're here to help fight Ulstermen," the young man on the box called to her.

"I didn't come here to fight anybody," Eileen answered, feeling her own temper rise.

"Then you're against us as all the Donegans have been," a man in farmer's overalls cried out.

"I'm not against you or anybody," Eileen said.

"Then you're against us," someone else shouted. "Just more of the clever Donegan words, that's what. We don't need you over here to carry on again."

She looked at their faces, good faces made hard and unyielding by hate, by memories never left to die. "Look, here, I'm not being clever about anything," Eileen said.

"Traitor would be the better word," someone shouted. Eileen's temper exploded.

"How dare you call me names?" she shot back. "If you people spent half as much energy finding a peaceful way to solve problems, you wouldn't need any fighting."

"Peaceful be damned and you with it," a man called back. "It was guns not peace that won freedom for Ireland. It was pikes not peace that the croppies used to light the spark of freedom."

"That was then. Now is now," Eileen retorted. "Good God, haven't we learned anything? Are you all so involved with the past that you can't see things are different today? Bloodshed isn't an answer today. The problems can be solved peacefully, whatever they are."

Eileen heard more catcalls. "The House of Drumroe won't be standing in our way again," someone shouted, and Eileen desperately wished she knew what all the jeers and cryptic references meant. But she also knew that a hard core of angry determination had frowned inside her.

"Fighting, fighting, is that all you know?" Eileen asked the man on the box.

"It was good enough then and it's good enough now," he shouted back at her. She shook the flame of her head.

"No, it's never good enough," she countered. "There was probably a better way then, too, but nobody looked for it, just as you don't want to look for it now."

"Go home," a woman shouted. "We've had enough of the Donegan talk. We don't want to hear it."

The crowd rumbled and started to move toward her, and she felt fright, sudden fear. These people were caught up in the web of their own emotions, inflamed hatreds. There was no felling what they would do. Looking over their heads she saw the priest standing on the steps of the Church, and she walked toward him, into the midst of the crowd. The move took them by surprise and they fell back, opening a path for her reluctantly. She heard angry comments and mutterings as she continued through them, and then she saw a girl with long black hair staring at her. As Eileen drew close the girl waited and then moved away, her walk a long, slithering stride, her large breasts thrust out voluptuously, and Eileen's mind flashed back to the scene on the mountain. It was the same girl, she was sure of it. And the girl's eyes had bored into her with a look that could well have been recognition. But she was at the church steps now and the girl had gone off with the crowd as it dispersed in the small market square.

"Difficult times are upon us again, Miss Donegan," the priest said, and Eileen saw he was a thin man with tired eyes.

"More difficult because of their ideas, Father," Eileen said. "What do you say to them?"

"I try to stay out of it, my child," the priest said. Eileen felt her impatience gathering. "To stay out of it is to encourage them," she said.

"There's wrong on both sides," he said. Eileen held her temper, but just barely. He was using piousness to cloak his own inadequacies or his own silent agreement. She saw weakness and confusion in the man, perhaps reflected from the times, but nonetheless there. Her own anger demanded more of the man than he could or would give, and her patience was short.

"The people don't listen anymore, not the way they used to," the priest said, and the girl ignored the pain in his eyes. "The role of the Church is different today," he said.

"Not the role, only the emphasis," Eileen shot back. "Its role is still to show the right from wrong, to lead and not to back away."

"How can one lead when no one follows?"

"How can they follow when no one leads?" she countered tartly, turning on her heel and striding away. There was indeed a troubled land here. Rory Muldoon had not exaggerated. She walked on till she found the street with the small sign that said KIELY STREET. There was but one white-walled house on it and she knocked at the door. Rory opened the door and brought her into a small room with a single desk and a phone. A few books took up a short shelf, and two chairs were the remainder of the furnishings. He certainly didn't go in for elaborate offices, she mused silently. But his smile, rakish, charming, and his sandy hair falling loosely over his forehead brightened her at once, and she plunged into telling him of her premonition about Aunt Agnes and about the incident with the old mullagh man. He seemed to brush everything aside, but she saw the concern in his eyes when she spoke of her vision in the night.

"Premonitions," he said thoughtfully. "Terrible things they can be. I'm glad you told me you've often had them and how they've been so right. That puts an entirely new light on things, now doesn't it?"

Her brow furrowed and he went on quickly. "Well, now you've real reason to stay. You've got to find out if your premonition was right. If it was, you'll want to know and carry through whatever has to be done. If it wasn't, you'll want to know that, too."

"I'm glad to hear you say that because that's exactly how I feel about it," Eileen said. "Where are the papers I'm to sign?"

Rory gave her a quick glance she couldn't read and then a wide, dazzling smile as he bent low to look into her eyes. "I'll have to keep watching you to see that you don't get into any more trouble," he said.

"And the papers?" she persisted. He straightened up and became all business at once.

"Let me check them over once more and I'll bring them to you in a day or two," he said. "Meanwhile, I think you need a change of pace, something to let you enjoy this fine country. How about a picnic tomorrow?"

"That would be fun," Eileen thought aloud.

"And it'll give me a chance to enjoy myself while keeping an eye on you. There's a magnificent spot where you can see right across the water to Aran. The *shantully,* the old hillock, it's called. I'll pick you up at eleven."

"I can't promise to be a carefree companion," Eileen said. "I can't stop thinking about Lady Donegan."

"We'll do our best," he said gallantly. "Shall I see you back to the house?"

"No, I'm all right," she answered. "In fact, I'd like to walk alone for a spell. Anyway, the meeting in the square was breaking up as I left it."

Rory pressed her hand reassuringly, and she went out into the streets, the neat, winding village streets so very lovely and hiding so much turmoil and anger. As she walked back through the town, aware that now most of those she passed were ignoring her, she searched for the girl with the long black hair and the distinctive walk. But the girl had gone and was nowhere to be seen. Had the girl really recognized her? It was one more worry to add to the sizable collection she was gathering. The day was into the afternoon already and she walked slowly up the road that curved into sight of Drumroe, rising up with its stark beauty. It seemed to look down at the land with an unyielding hatred of its own, an arrogance that had no right to come out of stone and metal and wood. Yet it did, and the girl shuddered in the sun. Her eyes swept up to the little cemetery on the hill and the frown was on her brow again until she wiped it away angrily.

Molly was in the kitchen and heard her come in.

"No word from Lady Donegan yet," the cook called out. Eileen nodded and walked to the kitchen. She had ceased to expect any word, but she didn't tell Molly that. The salmon, with the head removed, lay on a strip of cheesecloth which Molly was preparing to wrap it in. Eileen stayed to help a while. It took her mind from the dark and frightening thoughts that kept racing around inside it. She helped Molly place the salmon in a big iron kettle and watched as the cook added just enough water to cover the fish, and then seasoning of onion, parsley sprigs, vinegar, bay leaf, and salt and pepper. As the fish slowly began to cook in simmering water, Molly started to prepare the Erin sauce.

"What is Erin sauce?" Eileen asked. "From the things you have out here, I'd say it was a basic white sauce with special ingredients, sort of like an English parsley sauce except with spinach."

"A little, maybe," Molly said. "It's called by different names in different places. I've heard it called Irish green sauce, Spinach sauce, and Erin sauce. But spinach is the flavor ingredient and it's wonderful with any fish. Stay and I'll teach you how to make it."

It was a happy thought and the girl stayed, listening and watching the older woman who prepared the sauce with the practiced casualness of a professional. When she was finished, the time had come to go upstairs and prepare for dinner. Eileen hurried to the big room, again glad for Molly O'Connell's uncomplicated presence in Drumroe. Eileen took a warm bath and changed to a dress of deep blue that made the dark flame of her hair a living halo of fire. The deep scooped neck revealed the soft rise of her full breasts. She wanted information from Colin, if he had any to give, and she was shamelessly willing to make the most of her charms to get it. Molly showed her where the liquor cabinet was in the library, and Eileen had ice and glasses ready when he arrived. His smile was the quiet, reserved smile she had come to expect, with that steady, solid, reassuring quality in it. But his eyes, even when they lingered on the low scoop of her neckline, were grayer, colder, it seemed. Or was she just imagining things?

In any case, it was that contrast that made this man so compelling, the warm, contained smile and the gray blue, probing eyes. They talked over drinks in the library, and Eileen worked hard to keep the conversation on a light level until Molly announced dinner was served. Eileen was still working at it when they sat down in the huge, austere dining room, feeling very small in its vastness. But she paused, noticing the cool amusement in his eyes.

"You'll not enjoy the evening at all if you keep trying not to talk about whatever it is you want to talk about," he said, and she smiled, sheepishly. He had a way of being uncomfortably accurate, and she quickly told him what had happened during her walk through Cladvale and of the girl with the long, black hair who she was sure recognized her. She passed over her visit with Rory. It wasn't important to what she wanted to learn from Colin. She watched a grimness creep into his eyes, turning them into a steel gray.

"There's little to be done about the girl now except to watch yourself," he said. "If she recognized you, she may be more frightened than you over it. And you're not certain, anyway."

He paused. "As for the incident at the market square, you didn't do much to calm things by arguing with them," he commented dryly.

"I guess not. I just couldn't help myself," Eileen said.

"Someone once said that red-haired women and gunpowder were alike in that it takes very little to make them explode,"

Colin commented, his eyes twinkling unexpectedly. "And now you want to know what some of the things that were shouted at you meant. I think I can help you there, having been giving a lot of study to the recent past of Drumroe."

She watched as he leaned back in his chair, letting his eyes roam over the dark walls and the paintings that hung in the big room as he spoke to her.

"During the uprising in 1918, Lady Donegan lived here with her mother and father," he began. "Most of the immediate family lived here then, or at least made Drumroe their official home. But Lady Donegan's father, Kenneth Donegan, was a sick man, and it was her mother, at that time Lady of Drumroe, who really ran things. It seems that the House of Drumroe has its own tradition which is one of peace. For centuries they have been what I guess we'd call pacifists today. Well, when the trouble broke out for real, the men of Drumroe refused to take part in it. And so did the women, of course. They tried, instead, to convince the patriots to come together with the English, to find some solution without a bloody uprising. Now, my girl, that's usually an unpopular role all around, and it was then, too. The pressures grew greater on your aunt's mother and the others as the fighting began in earnest. Fighting was going on all over, and then, as now, Drumroe is close to the border of Ulster where the raids and counterraids were particularly heavy.

"The Donegans refused to help either side and, though they weren't too popular with the Irish patriots, some of them gave Drumroe credit for holding to its beliefs."

Eileen paused in her listening to wonder if that were why she had such deep, unreasoned feelings about the present fighting. That business of what can be transmitted again, she murmured silently. But Colin was going on and she brought her attention back to him quickly.

"Things didn't touch Drumroe itself until one night in the late fall," he continued. "A man named Terence Malachy led the Fifth Irish Army Brigade in this area. Word got out that the British were sending in a force to wipe out the rebel hotbed here. Malachy gathered his men and attacked the English by the rising of the moon. But he had let himself be carried away by his own eagerness. The English had brought up two other brigades in the night, and they caught Terence Malachy and his force in a pincer movement. Malachy and his men had to run to escape death or capture, just about the same thing then. They would have escaped if they could have cut through the Donegan land, over the ridge, around the house of Drumroe itself. It was the one avenue for them. But the land had been closed by mines and by men hired by the Donegans. These men had orders to protect the neutrality of Drumroe and shoot anyone who violated it. In the mist of the night they didn't even know whether it was English soldiers or rebels disregarding the privacy of their land, but they shot at those trying to cross Drumroe land and the fleeing rebels had to go back. Of course, most of them were captured or killed by the English. Terence Malachy escaped. He was never heard from again, never found, and all sorts of rumors sprang up. Some said he was killed and just never found. Others said he was filled with bitter shame and fled Ireland thinking he had led his own men into a trap. I happen to know that he did flee Ireland, first in shame and fear, and then in bitterness. Half his face had been shot away and he lived out the rest of his life acting as a fence for stolen goods in England near Liverpool."

Colin paused, as though he were going to say more and had thought better of it. He left the matter of Terence Malachy and went on.

"Of course, you can see how the Donegans were hated then," he said. "Later, when the uprising had succeeded, when there were still many prisoners and hostages held by the English, Lady Donegan was the only negotiator able to secure the release of the Irish prisoners. In some people's eyes that partly vindicated the house of Drumroe. She was then in the unique position of being trusted by the English and grudgingly by the people of the now-free Ireland. But that partial vindication wasn't held by all, and it didn't wipe out the hatred and the blame most people placed upon the House of Drumroe for its original position. As you know, things don't die easily over here and certainly not among the country people. So you see, Eileen, the House of Drumroe has been a thing apart, as it was before that, when the so-called witch of Drumroe lived here."

"It's a sobering background," Eileen commented. "But I'm proud of it. The Donegan's stood for something better than senseless bloodshed, and they had the courage to stick to their principles. And they were good principles. It's not right that it should leave such a heritage of hate."

"No, it's not right. It's just so," Colin said. She saw his eyes studying her. "What are you thinking, Colin?" she smiled at him.

"I'm thinking it might be much better for you to leave here until all this is cleared up," he said.

"You, too?" she said and saw his eyebrows lift questioningly.

"Rory Muldoon started out by telling me that, too," she said. "But he's changed his mind now, after I told him of my premonition about Aunt Agnes. He agrees with me now that I've got to stay here and see this thing through. And that's what I'm going to do."

"Stubbornness," he grinned at her. "But I expected as much. Try and not do anything foolish though. No more running out in the dead of night following fife players."

His tone was condescending, as though she were a child. "I'll try and be careful," she said. "Rory Muldoon's taking me out on a picnic tomorrow, up to a spot called the shantully."

"Is he now?" Colin said and she was irritated by the cool amusement in his eyes. She'd wanted something else, perhaps a tinge of annoyance or jealousy. "I know the spot," he added. "It's very nice indeed. I'm a little surprised you're in a mood for picnicking, though."

Damn him, he'd hit back where it hurt, she knew. She answered honestly, her only defense. "I'm not. I thought it'd help take my mind off things."

She saw his eyes soften. "I hope it does," he said, and she was glad for the gentleness in his voice. "I'm going to be up that way myself tomorrow," he added. "There are some *souterrains* near there I want to look at."

He got to his feet, draining the glass of brandy she had poured him at the end of dinner, and Eileen felt his arm hook into hers as he turned for the door. "It's been grand," he said. "The most enjoyable evening I've had since I rented that little cottage. But then, the company makes all the difference."

He could indeed have the smooth charm of the Irish, she saw again, and she wondered what made her feel so uncertain of this big man. And yet so attracted to him. He held her hand for a moment as they stood at the door and she saw his eyes sweep the dark expanse of the lawn with a swift, probing glance.

"We must do it again soon," she said.

"It would be nice," he answered, his eyes soft, dancing, surprising her. "But you're entirely too beautiful a girl to be next to for long. It takes too much willpower."

"Next time don't bring so much," she tossed back at him.

"I promise not to," he said and she closed the door as he went down the roadway, disappearing into the dark. She had just closed the door when she heard the soft knock and opened it to find him there. "By the way," he said, almost casually. "I'd appreciate it if you'd let me know about anything that you find out concerning Lady Donegan."

"I will, Colin," she said and saw the gray blue eyes were hard again. She closed the door and leaned against it for a moment, wondering whether to be grateful or wary because of his interest. He was an intriguing man, Colin Riorden. Molly, on her way to her room in the other wing of the house, passed down the hall and Eileen waved to her. Then she walked to her own room, thinking of what Colin Riorden had told her. It had been more than mere history, and she thought again of her psychic transmissions, all those gifts or powers rooted somewhere in past ages and brought to her by some means. Was it possible that not agreeing with the times could be "in her blood," as Rory had phrased it. She had scoffed at the mere thought, but in the market square—facing the hostile crowd—she had felt her inner feelings crystallize with an intensity she had never known before. Was it possible that this, too, was some form of transmission? Or was it only past teachings of early childhood asserting themselves with a suddenness that made it seem more than it was?

She went to her purse and took the letter out again, a phrase in it suddenly flashing in her mind. The last lines of the paragraph blazed out at her, and as she read them again, Colin's story gave them new meaning. Suddenly they became not words but statements fraught with import and torn from the pages of history.

> Those who have been in line to take title to the House of Drumroe have all, over these past years, met with one unfortunate tragedy after another. *Perhaps, once, we were all guilty of a terrible wrong. I say perhaps because to this day I cannot make myself believe that.*

It was, indeed, all there in that one phrase, that whole tragic time Colin had told her about. A reflection of a searching conscience was there, too, and something more, a reaffirmation of faith in a stand once taken and held to despite all pressures. She scanned the letter again, looking for what else it might tell her, what else she had read but not seen. But, like the uncounted other times she had read it over, it revealed nothing specific. She put the letter back in her purse, undressed, and opened the tall windows a few inches. The night was warm and she lay down on the bed, naked, stretched across it at an angle so she could see the line of the red ridge and the silver glow of the moon behind the trees. The glow grew brighter as she watched, and soon the moon crested over the top of the ridge. She got up and stood at the windows, a slender, beautiful wraith in the darkness, pulled there by the silver sphere that rose in the sky. As she watched the rising of the moon she heard the silent, insistent voice inside her calling, urging, telling her in the words of Yeats, to "walk among long dappled grass, and pluck till time and times are done, the silver apples of the moon...."

As she stood there the sound of the fife drifted up to her, mournfully stirring, and out of the silvered dark the rest of the words of the song came to her:

"Out of many a mud-walled cabin,
    Eyes were watching through the night,
Many a manly heart was throbbing,
    For the coming morning's light.
Murmurs ran along the valley,
    Like the banshees mournful tune,
And a thousand pikes were flashing,
    By the rising of the moon."

She closed the window, shutting out the sound of the fife with effort. Laying down on the bed, she held herself very still as the strains of the song still echoed in her ears and the silver light of the moon filtered through the window over her. Her body trembled softly for a brief moment. The rising of the moon would come to mean still more to her. She knew not what it would mean, only that it would mean something. One of these mist-swept nights, by the rising of the moon, she would have the answer to that. She closed her eyes knowing it, as certain of it as she was of her own name. But wasn't even that a thing of uncertain meaning, she murmured as she fell asleep.

The morning sun swept into the room on warm yellow wings that lighted the fire of her hair and caressed the lovely rise of her breasts as she lay with the sheet more off than on her. By her watch on the small night table she saw she had overslept, and she dressed quickly, putting on brightly flowered hip-huggers and a sleeveless blouse. As she turned to go downstairs, she paused to gaze out over the ridge where she had seen the moon rise in the night. She hadn't forgotten the certainty that had come to her then, but she put it aside for now. She could only wait and, as she walked down the wide stairs, she realized that she had indeed found a new part of herself. She was facing the strange powers that moved within her without the selftorturing fear of them, or certainly with less of it. Even the searching that had so long been a part of her had changed character. She searched for even more answers now, but the aimless desperation was gone from it. Instead, there was an angry determination that was somehow vitalizing. Perhaps it took the unexplained scent of dark evil here to make her change her own inner self. She had known terror here and had trembled in fright, but it was a different kind of fright. She had found the difference between being afraid for herself and being afraid of herself.

Downstairs Molly was in the big hallway with a wicker picnic basket filled with things.

"I heard you talking to that Colin Riorden about your picnic when you were in the hall last night," the cook said. "So I got everything ready for you."

Eileen hugged the little woman to her impulsively. "You're an angel, Molly," she said. If it weren't for the terrible cloud of Aunt Agnes's continued absence, it could be a marvelous day, she knew. But the cloud was there and she knew that, too. "We're going to the shantully," she said to the little woman. "Do you know the spot?"

"Indeed, and a lovely spot it is," Molly said. "Though it's been a good many years since I've been there picnicking."

Eileen heard a door open and she turned to see Brannock standing there by the cellar entranceway. She was tempted to remark on people who listen behind doors, but she held her tongue as he walked past them, dour, his lined face expressionless. When he'd gone outside Eileen turned to Molly.

"Why did Lady Donegan ever hire him?" she exclaimed.

"Good handymen are hard to come by, especially here at Drumroe," Molly said. "There are a lot of folks who wouldn't work here."

Eileen thought of Colin's capsuled history of Drumroe and quickly understood why. "Besides, your aunt likes to take in stray cats," Molly added. At Eileen's questioning glance she went on. "Brannock had served a prison term for smuggling," Molly said. "Lady Donegan said that he'd paid his debt to society and there was no reason to deny him honest work. And, though he's not exactly lovable, he does do his work."

And what else, Eileen asked silently as Molly went back to the kitchen. She took the wicker basket and went outside to wait for Rory. He arrived a few minutes later in the little open-topped MG, and in moments they were heading down the road, skirting a donkey cart in a cloud of dust. Rory drove with a grim recklessness she decided, not at all in keeping with a proper solicitor. But then, that's what she liked about him, his air of reckless charm, of tightly wound energy. She wouldn't have liked a prim and proper solicitor, she knew. They drove for nearly an hour and finally halted half-way up a narrow roadway in a small cleared area before a cluster of trees.

"We walk from here," Rory said, taking the basket. "It's not that far." He led her down a path through the trees that rose sharply and then leveled off. Before her, Eileen saw a tiny, single-file rope footbridge across a deep, rock-filled gorge. Narrow wooden boards formed the floor of the bridge and the railings were of rope. The entire flimsy affair was fastened with rope to the steel poles set in the ground at both ends. Rory started over first, grinning back at her.

"It's really quite safe, even though it is primitive," he said. "No one has ever fallen from it yet, so far as I know."

Eileen, taking a deep breath, followed him over. The little bridge swayed as she stepped across it, and she only glanced down once at the deep gorge below. She was very happy to reach the other side and the firm ground. Her hands were red from holding so tightly to the rope railing of the bridge. Rory was walking on, and she caught up to him just as they reached a hillock, and before her the ocean and the outline of the Isle of Aran swept into view. It was a windswept and stark view full of wild beauty, and she sat down to enjoy it as Rory started to unload the wicker basket.

"Damn!" he said suddenly. "I left the wine in the car. A picnic's no good without wine, at least not to me. I'll go get it. It's not that far back. You can get the rest of the things out meanwhile."

"If I don't just sit here and look at the view," Eileen answered.

"None of that, my girl. You're here to work," he said and she watched him hurry off, looking very boyish with his sandy hair blowing in the wind. He was truly charming with that light way about him.

He was back soon enough, the wine in the crook of his arm, along with two glasses. The warm sun, the food and wine, and Rory's charm and wit made her happier than she had any right to be. They had eaten and she was feeling shamefully lazy, determined not to think of all the fearful things still unanswered. Rory's hand was over hers as she lay back on the grass. It had been a long while since she'd held hands with anyone, and the sense of touch brought back remembered pleasures. Suddenly he leaped to his feet. "It's getting blasted hot here," he said, pulling her up. "Let's go over in the shade of the trees."

She bent down to gather up the wicker basket and the litter of their picnic when she heard his cry of pain. Whirling, she saw the rock skid out from under his foot and his body twist as he grabbed at his left knee with both hands. He was on the ground instantly, holding his knee, his face twisted with pain.

"Damn the luck!" he swore and she was beside him, her dark blue eyes wide, concerned. "A trick knee," he said drawing his breath in sharply. "Any damn thing can make it go out. I stepped on that rock and twisted the wrong way. It's a memento from my Rugby days."

Eileen wanted to touch it but she held back, afraid to hurt him more. "Can I pull on it or something?" she asked, feeling helpless. He shook his head. "No, it'll take a few days to go back into place again," he said. "But I have to keep it tightly wrapped. I carry a role of that rubberized bandage for times like these. You know the stuff that's used for sprains and pulled muscles."

"Yes, in America it's called an Ace bandage," she said. "Where is it, at your office?"

"No, I keep a role in the dashboard of the car," he said. "I never know when the damned thing will do this on me."

"You stay right here," Eileen said. "I'll get it and be right back." Rory's eyes looked up at her gratefully.

"Would you?" he said. "Wonderful. It'd be bloody slow going back this way. Once it's bandaged I can hobble along quite well."

"I'll only be minutes," she said, hurrying off. His rakish grin followed her despite the obvious pain of his leg. She half-ran down the little pathway through the trees and halted as she came to the little footbridge over the gorge. Stepping carefully onto it, she felt it sway with her every step as it had the first time. She was almost half over it, her hands hurting again from clutching the rope railing so tightly, when she felt it shudder and the swaying changed to something else. The rope railing in her hand went slack and she looked back to see the rope tear away from the metal supporting rods. She heard her scream of pure terror as she felt herself plunging into the gorge. Her hands reached out, caught the rope of the bridge as it swung and she swung with it, clinging with terrified desperation. She saw the stone wall coming at her as the torn bridge, still secured by the far end, swung across the gorge. She managed to take a tighter grip of the rope as she was slammed into the stone. Her body shook with pain from the impact, but she clung to her grip. She reached her other hand up and got a better hold. She was hanging with the little bridge against the far wall, the rest of the footbridge dangling beneath her. She screamed for help and heard her cry echoing through the gorge. She could feel her strength waning quickly and she wrapped her legs around the rope. It helped a little, but she knew it would not last long.

    Eileen screamed again and again as she felt her hands giving out. She managed to wrap her wrist half-way around the thick rope to relieve some of the pressure on her cramped, stiffened fingers, but as the footbridge swayed gently with her dangling against it like a giant fly, she felt herself start to slip. Tightening her legs around the rope, she pulled herself up an inch. It was enough to change her position slightly and give her another moment to cling to life. But the moments were being used up, she knew, and she screamed again, hearing the desperate terror in her voice. She looked up at the other wall where the rope had torn loose from the supports and she saw his head, the sandy hair falling down over his forehead. He was on his stomach, crawling to the edge, looking down over it.

    "Rory!" she screamed and she saw he looked down at her in helplessness. Suddenly she realized that he might just as well not have pulled himself back at all because he could be of no help to her. Even if his knee were in place and he could run, there was no way to reach her from that side. By the time he found his way to help it would be too late. She was growing nauseous from weakness now, and only the cramped muscles of her hands, grasping like clawed talons, held her there. They would give out soon, she knew, in a sudden release that would send her plunging to her death. Rory's head was still looking down at her and then she saw him pull back, heard the sound of his body as he pulled himself along the ground. Then she heard the other voice from directly above her.

"Hold on," the voice said and she craned her neck upward to see Colin Riorden on the edge above. "I'm going to pull you up. You just hold tight."

He didn't expect an answer, she knew. Besides, she hadn't the strength left to even nod. She felt the dangling rope move, felt herself being pulled upward with it, scraping along the stone wall of the gorge. He pulled slowly, pausing with every third or fourth pull. But the edge was coming closer, almost within reach now. However, she dared not reach out. Her cramped muscles wouldn't permit it. Then she felt Colin's hands on her, pulling her over the top of the ledge, and she was laying there in his arms, her breath coming in long, shallow drafts. Finally, she moved to sit up and he let her go.

"Thank you," she said, hearing how absolutely, ridiculously inadequate it sounded. His eyes were looking past her, across the gorge and she turned to see Rory there on the ground.

"Bloody well done, Riorden," he called. Eileen looked back at Colin who had gotten to his feet. He reached down and pulled her up. She wanted to bury herself in his arms, and yet she had a terrible feeling of uncertainty, of fright.

"You'd said you would be nearby," she commented. "I'm glad you were this close."

"I heard your screams," he said. "When I got a bearing on them and got here your friend across the way was just crawling to the edge, too. We saw each other at the same time. I just happened to be on the right side to pull you up."

Eileen smiled gratefully and felt a hypocrite. Why did he just happen to be on the right side to pull her up? How did he happen to be so many places at such opportune times? They were shameful thoughts, but she wasn't turning away from anything any longer. She'd think more about them later. Now she turned to where Rory was sitting up, one hand on his knee.

"There's another way down, a long way," he said. "It comes out at the bottom of the gorge. I'll crawl down it. Take me a good hour at least, I'd guess."

"I know where it is," Colin called. "We'll take your car and drive there and meet you."

Rory waved and she followed Colin to where the MG waited. "My car's down on the other end of the gorge," he said, taking out a set of keys and putting one into the ignition. "I've an MG at home," he explained with a smile.

Eileen put her head back and let the wind blow through her hair, grateful to be able to feel it, to be alive. "Close call, that," Colin commented. "I think you're accident-prone, Eileen Donegan."

"Maybe," she said. "I've enough strange things about me. Why not that, too?"

They drove the rest of the way in silence and reached the bottom of the gorge almost a half hour before Rory came crawling down, his clothes muddy and caked with leaves. She ran to him at once and helped him into the car. He opened the dash and brought out the roll of bandage. After wrapping it expertly around his knee, he drove Colin back to his car.

"Hell of a way to end a picnic," Rory commented ruefully. He looked at Colin. "It would have been a worse ending if you hadn't come by just then. Thanks, again."

Colin nodded, his smile slow and easy, and his eyes just flickered over hers, Eileen saw. But she caught the cool reserve in them. Seeing them together this way, Colin and Rory, the contrast between them was that much stronger. Rory seemed completely his easygoing, rakish self, but there seemed a certain inner tension about Colin. Or was she imagining that? There always was some of that about him, only now there seemed a little more. She watched him get into his car with a wave, and then she was driving home with Rory. He drove even faster this time, but she didn't mind. She was anxious to get home, too. Dark thoughts were whirling around inside her, and a grim anger gathered as she thought back over what had happened. Too many strange things were happening here and they couldn't all be coincidences.

They couldn't all be explained away so rationally, and again she thought of the first night by the lough and the red lantern which vanished. Rory had given her a reasonable possibility to explain that, but suddenly she wasn't interested in any explanations. She wanted to know for herself, to see with her own eyes, to find her own proof.

When they reached Drumroe she was quietly excited. Rory had been a dear and he looked drawn, tired, disheveled. She kissed his cheek lightly. "You go straight home," she said. "I'll call you later and see how you are."

"I'll be at that office number," he said. "I'm damn glad you're alive." He put the car into gear and roared away. Eileen watched him go and then hurried to the garage. She got into the powerful old Jaguar again and drove out of the garage and down the road she had just come with Rory. It would still be light when she got there, she calculated, and she kept a steady pace on the almost deserted late-afternoon roads. Finally she was back at the small clearing. She got out of the car with a quick bound and hurried up the little path through the cluster of trees. The gorge loomed ahead of her and she saw the bridge on the ground where Colin had pulled it. Kneeling down, she examined the end that had come loose. It may have been nothing save unreasoned, wild suspicion on her part, but she had to know. She'd had it with strange accidents. The end of the rope was stiff and twisted where it had been knotted and twined around the steel supports. Half of it was shredded and torn where it had given way. But, with a gasp, she saw that the other half of the knotted end had been severed cleanly. It had been cut partially through so that anyone's weight on the little footbridge would have been enough to tear away the rest. It had been no accident, but cleverly contrived attempted murder. And it would have been successful, too, if Colin hadn't come along. If she and Rory had gone back across the little bridge together, they'd both have been killed, hurtled into the gorge. But it wasn't Rory who was the target. It had been she.

Trembling in mixed fear and anger, she got up and went back to the car. She wanted to get back to Drumroe, to the silence of her room. She had a lot to think about and try to put together, and she would not turn away from anything.

Eileen drove fast, faster than Rory had driven, but it was dark by the time she reached the great monster of a house and put the car in the garage. Before going to her room she stopped in the library and called Rory. He answered after a few rings and caught the tension in her voice at once.

"What is it, Eileen?" he asked.

"More than I'm going to go into now," she said, half-whispering into the phone. "But that accident was no accident this afternoon. Just answer this for me. Did you tell anyone we were going up to the shantully on a picnic?"

She heard his pause as he thought. He answered slowly.

"I guess I did mention it when I bought the wine from Mr. Connighan," he said. "There were a few other people there."

"Was one of them a girl with long, streaming black hair and big breasts?" Eileen asked.

"You mean the O'Mally girl?" he said. "She's the only one that fits that description. Yes, come to think of it, she was there. And so was Kenny Monahan and old McGill."

"Did you speak to anyone else after that?"

"Not a soul," he replied. Her lips in a tight line, she thanked Rory and hung up, not giving him time for questions. She went to her room, slipped on the lock and lay down in the darkness. Slowly, carefully, she assembled the facts. First, rising up in monstrous reality now, was the collapse of the little footbridge. It had been no accident and she was not, as Colin had suggested, accident-prone. She was murder-prone. That night by the lough, when the tree had almost killed her, had been no accident, either. The red lantern had been placed so she would stop just where she had, where the tree could crash down upon her. Whoever had done it had seen the car go into the lough and thought the terrible deed had been accomplished. It would have simply been a tragic accident, just as the footbridge was intended to be. To even dream of a motive was beyond her imagination. Why should anyone want to kill her? The motive, whatever it was, had to be connected with her coming here to Drumroe, to Aunt Agnes. Her conviction that Aunt Agnes was dead was now deepened by the word murder. Whatever had happened to her aunt had not been by accident, either.

Eileen got up, took off the blouse and slacks, and lay back across the bed, her mind racing, returning to the picnic with Rory. Who had known they were going there, to that spot where they would need to cross the little footbridge over the gorge? Brannock had known. He had heard her discussing it with Molly. She dismissed Molly at once, but Brannock's gaunt face stayed in her mind. The man hated her presence there. It was in his every glance. Enough to murder her? Possibly, she realized, very possibly. Perhaps he was involved in something he feared Aunt Agnes had discovered, and might have told her about. And he knew of her arrival, he'd seen her cable to Aunt Agnes. Brannock was indeed a more than likely suspect. Of course, Colin knew she would be at the shantully with Rory and she recalled the shocked surprise on his face when she had met him beside the lough on that morning after she'd plunged into the water. Was he surprised to see her alive? Yet today he had saved her at the gorge and that didn't fit in at all. He needed only to go away and she would have fallen in another minute. She felt her brow crease as she recalled what he'd said then. He'd said that he and Rory had reached opposite sides of the gorge at the same time. That could explain his saving her, she mused grimly. If he had come up to see the results of his handiwork and there was Rory across the way watching him, looking across at him, he would have had to save her.

She found herself almost sick with a sour, bitter knot in her stomach. It just couldn't be Colin, she told herself. He could have done away with her that night when she'd stumbled into his cabin. Or could he have, she wondered grimly, examining every possibility. The murderer was taking no chances, taking great pains to make certain everything seemed as though it were an accident. Just doing away with her at the cottage might have seemed too risky. Damn, Eileen swore to herself. Stop speculating about Colin, she told herself. The black-haired girl had known. She'd heard it in the store, a perfect opportunity to strike. She could have set the scene for the *accident*. Or the girl could have gone to the old mullagh man and told him she had recognized the Donegan girl and was afraid. He would have had time to come to the shantully, using his mountain shortcuts. There had been plenty of time to partially sever the rope after Rory had returned with the wine. They had eaten leisurely, talked, and let the afternoon slide by. Indeed, there had been plenty of time for anyone to have done it, perhaps even some half-witted idiot from the village triggered by her presence here at Drumroe.

But Eileen didn't favor that theory. Whoever did it had also tried to kill her that night beside the lough when she first arrived. That would include Brannock, of course, and anyone with whom he might be involved. The possibilities were endless, and she was going around in circles. If, as Rory had suggested, the attack by the lough had not been intended for her, then the list of suspects grew at once, no longer confined to those who'd known of her coming.

Eileen rose, slipped off her bra and panties, and lay down on the bed again, trying to find sleep while her mind continued to whirl with thoughts and probing questions. The killer had struck once at least, probably twice, and he would strike again. A grim anger was shouldering the fright she felt. There was more than murder here in this sweet land. There was evil, pure evil. It had struck at her aunt first and now at her. It was so real she could almost feel it, and she turned and buried her face into the pillow.

Where was that gift of the damned now when she needed it? Where was that blinding vision to see things she had never seen?

She'd asked the question before and the answer was always the same. It was a gift not really hers, neither to command nor to will, not to control in any way. If she were to stay alive, she would have to find the way herself.

She had come here to find new meanings out of the past, she reminded herself. She had come to find herself. Perhaps she was doing just that. Perhaps she first had to stare death in the face, to overcome it or lose forever. Perhaps this was her own test of fire. She lay still and felt her body finally grow less tense until sleep came to her, a restless, fitful sleep torn by anguished thoughts.

CHAPTER SIX

EILEEN WOKE with the first sun and dressed quickly. The bitter truth of what she faced was still upon her. There was really no way for her to begin, no way to seek out an unknown killer. She was almost forced to wait, to let him strike again. Yet she couldn't just sit back and wait till death reached out for her, especially when the third time might succeed. She'd tell Rory what she had found out, but no one else. It would be best if he killer did not know she suspected. Perhaps he could be coaxed into a wrong move. With Rory, she would try to work out some plan. Downstairs, Molly greeted her in the hall and brought her into the kitchen where a pot of tea and orange muffins were waiting.

"I spoke to Mrs. Mulcahey last night," Molly said. "I heard about your accident at the old footbridge by the shantully. You must still be frightened out of ten years growth."

"News travels around here," Eileen commented. But she knew that already.

"Thank God for that Mr. Riorden being in the right spot at the right time," Molly said. Eileen nodded. She was thankful for that and she thought of the big, quiet man with the cool eyes and sense of strength. She wanted to go to him, to really thank him, if only the dark thoughts weren't there. But they were, and she could not turn away from them. Not anymore. She finished breakfast and went into the warm sunlight outside. Brannock passed, his arms filled with cut firewood, and she watched him go by. She walked around to the rear of the house, her footsteps leading her up to the little hill and the cemetery. She was almost at the top when she saw Colin Riorden's figure sauntering up the other side. He waved at her, his smile slow, warm.

"How are you feeling the morning after?" he said.

"I only start shaking when I think about it," she said.

"Old gravestones your hobby?" he asked casually.

"No, in fact I've come up here to look at that one, Lady Donegan's," she said. "I saw it yesterday, and something about it made me frown. It disturbed me and I don't know why."

"And now?" he questioned. She felt her brow furrow.

"It still bothers me," she said. The bright green grass bordering the square bed of violets—the same lovely sight they had been yesterday. The violets in the foreground lifted upward to drink in the sun, more rich blue than violet in the brilliant light.

"Looks very nice to me," Colin said quietly.

"To me, too," Eileen said, turning away.

"But I am getting worried about Lady Donegan," he said. "Any more visions, hunches, anything?"

Eileen shook her head. "She's dead," she said softly. "That's all I know." She almost said murdered, but she held her tongue. He said it for her and she felt herself stiffen.

"And you think not by accident," he said softly. Her lips were tight and she managed to shrug.

"You disagreed with me," she countered, looking into his eyes. They were steady, unsmiling, holding her gaze.

"I did," he said. "And I still say murder isn't that easy to pull off. Have you thought of sending out a general alarm for your aunt?"

Eileen stared at him, her eyes wide. She hadn't thought of that, she admitted to herself, knowing he'd read as much in her eyes. "Maybe I still hoped against hope she would turn up," she said. "Maybe I wanted my premonition to be wrong."

"Let's still hold to that hope," Colin said and his hand was holding her arm. There was such a strength in his touch, reassuring steadiness. It almost made her heartsick. She wanted to tell him everything she had discovered, to confide in him. But she held back. She had to. It was a strange feeling to stand before a man who had saved her life and to wonder if he had saved it only to try to take it again. She decided to tell him one thing, though.

"I saw the girl from the druidic sacrificial ceremony," she said. "I think she recognized me."

"Don't go wandering off by yourself after dark," he answered, almost casually, one of the abrupt changes she had seen before in him.

"I won't," she said tartly. He nodded to her and she watched him go back over the hill. His eyes had turned stone gray and cold again. He was a strange man, she remarked silently. Casting another glance at the lovely square bed of violets, she paused for an instant and then left and hurried to the garage. Taking the powerful old Jaguar, needing the strength of it in her hands, she drove to Cladvale and Rory's little office. He opened the door for her, and she saw him limp to his chair by the desk.

"It's really not too bad," he grinned at her. "More of a damned inconvenience than anything else. But your remark over the phone last night shook me a bit. What did you mean?"

She opened her mouth to speak when he held up his hand. "Let's go upstairs," he said. "I've my living quarters there, just a room and a kitchen and bath, but there's a sofa and it'll be more comfortable. I don't expect anyone in today."

She followed Rory as he led the way to a small, steep staircase hidden behind the edge of the wall partition, out of sight. Upstairs, the room was indeed small, cramped, taken up mostly by the sofa, a lamp, and a small table. He stretched his leg out straight as he sat down on the sofa and she crowded into the corner next to him.

"Someone tried to kill me yesterday at the footbridge," she said bluntly. "I'm terribly sorry you got into it. You might have been killed along with me had we gone back together later."

Rory's incredulous eyes transfixed her. She told him everything she had discovered, and he listened intently. When she finished, telling him she was convinced the accident by the lough was an attempt to kill her, too, his jaw was tight, his face strained.

"Have you told anyone else about this?" he asked her.

"No, I thought it best not to," she said. "I'm hoping the killer will think I don't suspect and make a mistake."

"Good thinking, that," Rory said. "You've given me a list of people you have to include as possible suspects. I'll see what I can track down on every one of them. But it will take time, and there's danger in time. I don't want you going out alone at night without telling me where or when."

"About Colin Riorden," she said, hearing the hesitancy in her voice. "I don't really suspect him, and yet I do. I'm very confused about him."

"From now on we suspect everybody," Rory said. "I'll try to get a line on everyone's movements over the last forty-eight hours as a start."

"How can you do that?" Eileen asked.

"There are ways," he said. "You leave that to me."

His eyes smiled at her, and she was so happy to know at least someone was with her. She leaned forward and suddenly his lips were on hers, insistent, bold, his hands moving along her breasts. She felt the flame of desire, long denied, flare at once, and she was kissing him back, crushing herself against him. Finally she pulled herself away, knowing that no matter how warm and safe and wonderful it was in his arms, the time for that wasn't right yet.

"When this is over with," she said huskily. She saw his smile, crooked, a rueful quality to it, his eyes holding a secret laughter all his own. She stood up and he pulled himself to his feet.

"If I stay on, will you be my solicitor?" she asked jokingly.

"You won't stay on," he said and surprised her by the harshness of his tone. She smiled inwardly. He was preparing himself for the disappointment he felt was bound to come.

"By the way, how long have you been Aunt Agnes's solicitor?" she asked as he went down the steep stairway with her.

"Quite a long time," he said. "Long enough to know what's best for you and Drumroe."

"I'm sure," she said, kissing him lightly and then hurrying out the door. The weight didn't seem as heavy now that Rory was helping her. She got into the car and drove off, beyond Cladvale, just driving, following the winding roads wherever they took her, wandering under the warm sun. She was surprised at how quickly the day went and how far she had driven when she turned around to return to Drumroe. In the lush green and soft gold of the land it seemed inconceivable that a murderer stalked, seeking her life. It was hardly less conceivable to think that men were plotting and planning to rise up in arms, deciding on ways to best slay their countrymen. In the North, of course, other men were doing the same thing, a kind of silent madness that would explode into blood and pain of a sudden night. Would her life explode into blood and pain also? Is that what the rising of the moon would bring her? Would death find her then?

Eileen turned the questions over in her mind, questions at once burning and remote, real and so horrible that they seemed unreal. Had she returned here for a kind of appointment with destiny? The car turned a corner and she found herself on a lonely road which rose alongside the face of a mountain. She felt a cool wind, the hair on the back of her hands stood up, and suddenly she felt she was being watched. She looked around her, but she saw no one. The open-topped car and her burnished copper hair would be easy enough to spot, she knew. The feeling grew inside her, as that first night when she had driven from Shannon to Drumroe. The road rose higher and then leveled off, but wound and turned along the side of the mountain. She realized that she was lost. As soon as she got off this road she'd stop and get directions back to Cladvale. She slowed at a curve and, as the powerful throb of the Jaguar's engine cut to a murmur, she thought she heard the sound of another car behind her. She glanced back but saw nothing; a curve just behind her shut out the rest of the road. She had only turned another curve when she saw the figure standing on the rock just above the road, the long beard and robes moving in the wind. It was the old mullagh man and he saw her as she saw him. She knew she should speed up and go on, but she was tired of running, of waiting for fear to erupt into something worse. Perhaps she would eliminate him as a suspect or make him more of one. She reached down under the seat, her hand groping for something to use as a weapon, and she felt her fingers curl around a heavy tire wrench. She slowed the car to a halt just below the rock where he stood; she got out, holding the tire wrench in one hand, half-hidden behind the door. He was an old man and with the weapon she was not afraid. Not very afraid, anyway.

The old mullagh man stepped from the rock, disappearing behind it for a moment and then emerging on the road. His eyes were lighted with a fierceness, a fire that seemed more than human. As he stopped in front of her she saw he was a huge man, much larger than he had seemed from atop the rocks that night. Her throat dry, she took a firmer hold on the wrench she held behind her.

"I curse you for coming back," he said, and his voice was a low roar with the sound of falling rocks in it. "Harridan! Spoor of the Witch of Drumroe! It was foretold she would return with her red hair and her spying ways."

"Spying ways," Eileen echoed. "Then the girl told you, didn't she? She recognized me." Eileen felt her heart pounding suddenly.

"Yes, she told me!" the old mullagh man thundered. "But you'll not live to spy on anyone here. You'll not bring your terrible visions again. You'll not work your witching here."

"I'm no witch," Eileen said, trying to keep the fear out of her voice. The big, fierce-eyed man glared down at her, and she felt as though he could reach out and strike her down with one sudden blow. Her thought in stopping him was dissolving into a disastrous move.

"The witch is in all the Donegan women," he thundered.

"Nonsense," Eileen said. "I don't believe in witches. Poor Monica Donegan was no witch, either. Superstition had her killed. What did she do to be called a witch? I'll bet you don't even know."

The man's eyes burned with an even fiercer light as he glared down at her. "You know full well what she did," he thundered. "You'll not trick me. You know she foretold the plague that all but wiped out the valley. She told of it on one dark and stormy night. She saw death, she said, and a terrible plague. Then, when no one believed her, she brought it down upon the land till people died like flies in the sun. When they begged her for help, for mercy, she told them she did not bring the plague, that she could do nothing. Only after she was burned did the plague come to an end."

Eileen's mind raced as she listened to the old mullagh man's words. Monica Donegan had been subject to clairvoyance, to premonitions, just as she was. Monica had told them what she had seen—her vision of the plague, and, of course, they blamed her for it then. But poor Monica could not stop it anymore than she could stop the premonitions that had come to her. Monica Donegan had been no witch at all. Or else, and Eileen shrank from the thought, she herself was also one. If that be witchcraft, then she certainly qualified, and she was grateful she lived now and not in 1790.

"I'm not here to spy on you," Eileen said to the big, bearded, fierce-eyed man. "I didn't mean to be there the other night."

"You spied and you will pay for it," he intoned, his sonorous voice ringing out. Eileen got ready to come around with the heavy tire wrench, but the old mullagh man turned on his heel and strode back to the rock. He climbed up on it, and looked down at her for a long moment, while he seemed to be chanting a druidic curse. Then he turned again and started up the mountainside. Eileen watched him go, dropping the wrench onto the seat and flexing her fingers. Every few yards he would turn and stare down at her. Eileen was hypnotized, moving to the fender of the car to watch him, to make certain he continued on his upward journey. Like a bearded mountain goat, he moved up the side of the rocky mountain until he was but a tiny figure in the late afternoon shadows. Intent on watching the old mullagh man, she suddenly heard the noise behind her, soft footsteps on the dirt, the dry crunch of a twig. She started to whirl, but hands grabbed her from behind, one around her mouth, the other going around her neck, an arm tightening on her larynx. She couldn't move her head, couldn't see who was choking her, but her breath was quickly being squeezed from her. The one hand was still over her mouth, but she managed to get her lips open, and her teeth came down hard on the skin and muscle between the thumb and the forefinger. She felt the warm taste of blood in her mouth but, fighting off the nausea, she hung onto her grip. The hand tore away from her teeth, and she felt a blow on her temple as the arm moved from her windpipe. She was herself falling forward, the world swimming dizzily in front of her. Another blow came down hard against the side of her neck, and her face slammed into the dirt. Before she lost consciousness she imagined she heard the deep growl of a truck engine as it labored up a grade.

She lay there, unconscious, returning to the world as she felt her cheek being slapped firmly but gently. She opened her eyes, instantly ready to scream or claw for her life, but the big face before her was round and full of concern.

"There now, that's better," she heard the man say, and her eyes, focusing on more than his face, saw the big stake truck alongside the Jaguar. She let him pull her to her feet, clutching a big, powerful arm.

"What happened?" she asked, seeing she was alone with the truck driver.

"I was about to ask you that, Miss," he said. "I came up the grade and saw you lying there alongside your car."

She could feel the terrible, choking pressure upon her throat as she ran a hand over her neck. "Did you see anyone else?" she asked. "Another car down the road?"

"Well, yes, there was a car pulled off the road just the other side of the bend," the driver said.

"What kind of a car?" she asked quickly.

"Frankly, I didn't take much notice of it," he said. "But what happened here to you?"

She knew that any attempt at the truth would only make the good man think her mad, so a lie was more plausible than reality and she used it quickly.

"I was feeling dizzy so I stopped and got out," she said. "I guess I just fainted. A friend was supposed to be driving this way, but apparently he isn't coming. That's why I asked about the car. Could I follow you along? I'm going back to Cladvale."

"I'll pass within five miles of it," he said. "You're sure you're all right, now?"

She nodded, tossing him a reassuring smile. She got into the car and swung in behind the truck. It would be slow traveling but safe. Keeping one eye on the rearview mirror, she looked back for a glimpse of a car, but there was none. She had felt eyes on her, felt she was being watched. The old mullagh man could have been watching her from his rocky perch when she first swung onto the winding mountainside road. But there had been other eyes, and once more she had cheated death. Only the truck laboring up the grade had saved her this time, forcing the would-be killer to flee. Otherwise, she would have been the victim of an accident, found in her car which had plunged off one of the steep cliffs. And once more, almost anyone could have followed her. She had been the idle wanderer, not thinking that death was shadowing her, not in the soft sunlight of the day. But this time she could eliminate the old mullagh man from suspicion. But even as she gave the thought room, she knew she had to draw it back again. He had stood there for her to see, perhaps certain she would stop. He could have been giving someone else a chance to sneak up behind her, perhaps even the black-haired girl. The arm around her throat shutting the breath from her could have belonged to anyone, a man or a strong country girl. No, she told herself in grim anger, she could cross no one off the list.

When they neared Cladvale she recognized the road by the lough and signaled with her horn. The truck driver waved an arm at her as he sped off in the other direction. It was nearly dark and she drove along the road without slowing as she passed the little cottage. A light was on inside. Colin was there, but that meant nothing. He'd had more than enough time to get back. They'd all had time to fade into the shadows again. When she turned into the driveway of the great house, her brush with death returned to make her knees weak. She wanted only to lie down and gather herself. She'd take a moment to call Rory, though. She had to confide in someone and was grateful for his presence only a few minutes away.

As she parked the car in the garage she met Brannock carrying some shovels to the adjoining toolshed. Passing close to the tall, gaunt man, her breath drew in sharply as she saw a fresh bandage between the thumb and forefinger and extending up along the back of his hand. She made her voice stay calm, casual.

"Hurt yourself?" she asked. He paused, his deep eyes staring her down.

"Sawing wood," he answered in a low growl. "Power saw sent a sliver flying. Went right into my hand."

"Take care of it," she said and proceeded on into the house. In the library she dialed Rory and felt a flood of warmth at the sound of his voice. She hurriedly told him what had happened and of the bandage on Brannock's hand.

"Incriminating, but not conclusive," he said carefully. "You poor girl. I know how you feel. You certainly have had too many close ones. For what it's worth, I saw your friend Colin Riorden drive past my place a few minutes after you left, going down the road you'd taken."

Eileen didn't need him to spell it out any more clearly. She put the phone down and hurried to her room, pausing only to tell Molly she was too tired to eat. Night had come and she stripped and took a warm bath. Afterward, clad only in the towel, she lay on the bed exhausted. Brannock, she mused. Was he the one? And Colin had been driving, following down the road she had taken. He could have stayed discreetly behind her until he saw his opportunity. Before she fell asleep she had decided one thing. She wouldn't wait any longer. She'd make some moves of her own in the morning, and the first one would be to go through Aunt Agnes's personal papers. She had held back from doing so, but she had no choice now. Perhaps there would be something there which could help her. She fell asleep with the towel still wrapped around her, her body refusing to let her mind keep it awake any longer.

In the morning the smell of hot biscuits wafted up to her room, and she put on a full skirt and a pale green rayon jersey and hurried down to the kitchen. The cook set the jam and biscuits in front of her and Eileen ate well, surprised that she could eat at all. Her nerves were stretched thin, and she was tense with the thought of what she had to do.

"Where does Aunt Agnes keep her personal papers, Molly?" Eileen asked, realizing that she could not bring herself to use the past tense despite the certainty of what she felt.

"In her room, in the desk there. It's on the second floor a few doors beyond yours," the cook said. "If you've finished, I'll show you."

Eileen got up, pushing away her plate, and followed Molly as the little woman went up the stairs with her short-legged, bouncing gait. Aunt Agnes's room was almost regal, with royal blue walls and white drapes. A big four-poster bed with a white bedspread and royal blue pillows took up one corner. The chairs were deep and comfortable, and a full-length portrait of Kenneth Donegan, Aunt Agnes's father, hung on one wall. It was a room that suited the Lady Donegan Eileen remembered, somewhat severe but with a gracious, tasteful welcome about it. She saw the desk against the far wall and went to it at once.

"I may be up here a while, Molly," she said. "I don't want to talk to anyone but Mr. Muldoon if he calls."

"I understand," the little woman said as she closed the door on her way out. Eileen began to open the desk drawers, systematically going through each one. She found ledgers upon ledgers, some filled with household expenses, others with income from investments. Drumroe, indeed, just about balanced expenses against income, she found as she reached the most recent ledgers. But financial ledgers weren't what she sought. In one drawer she found a stack of neatly tied letters and she began to read them, one by one. They were mostly meaningless replies to personal messages Aunt Agnes had sent others. Some were answers to her aunt's letters of condolence when death had struck at the family. There were more papers, bills, statements, business correspondence. It took time to carefully go over each item, and she was despairing of ever finding anything when Molly called to say Rory was on the phone. She was glad for the interruption and surprised to see the morning had slipped into afternoon already.

Rory was concerned and solicitous, and she was glad to hear his voice. When she told him what she'd been doing, she heard him pause for a moment. "I wish you'd just not do anything but stay in the house and read," he said. "Let me try and track down something we can go on. Looking through your aunt's things will only depress you and upset you, and I doubt you'll find anything there."

He was right, of course. She had been depressed by going through Aunt Agnes's papers, by the unstated morbidity in the act. But just sitting around was impossible. She decided not to argue with Rory, though. He was trying so hard to help.

"You're sweet," she said. "Come see me if you can. That'll do me more good than anything else."

"I've got to go to Lifford today," he said. "I'll be back tonight. If it's not too late, I'll look in on you. You stay close to home."

He hung up and Eileen marched herself back to the big blue room at once. There was only one drawer left and she'd finish what she started. The big, leather-bound book inside it was a scrap book of newspaper photos, clippings, mementoes, theatre programs, all the very personal things a woman collects and keeps for reasons only she can explain. Eileen wanted to close it and not pry, but she knew that this might be the very thing she sought. As she went through the pages she found nothing, at least nothing she could connect with anyone. She was nearing the end of the large album when she paused at a newspaper clipping from the *Dublin Times*. A frown gathered on her brow as she read it quickly.

EVAN O'CANNON DIES—LEADING SOLICITOR. One of the leading solicitors in Ireland succumbed last night, a man who numbered many prominent people among his clients. Most of his clients had been with him since he began law practice and he had served them almost a lifetime. Among such lifelong clients were Herbert Hokins, Robert O'Boylesford, the Timothy Shannon Fund, Lady Agnes Donegan of Drumroe, and many others.

Eileen's eyes flew to the top of the page and the dateline there, May 4, 1969. She put down the obituary clipping and stared at the window alongside the desk. Then Rory had only been Aunt Agnes's lawyer for a short while, probably less than a year, only since the death of this Evan O'Cannon. But when she'd asked him that, he'd told her he'd been Aunt Agnes's solicitor for a long time. Why, she asked herself? Did even Rory stand in shadows? No, she answered angrily. There'd be a reasonable explanation. She was starting to see demons everywhere she looked and that was bad. Rory probably knew that if he told her he had only been Aunt Agnes's solicitor a short while, she wouldn't pay proper attention to his advice. That would be like him, she smiled, to anticipate her reactions.

She went back to the few remaining pages of the album. It was on the last page, empty except for a small slip of paper, that she found the name *Colin Riorden* in her aunt's handwriting. Three exclamation points followed the name. Eileen felt herself start to tingle. Why had her aunt scrawled this name with such emphasis on the slip of paper and stuck it away at the back of her personal album? What did it mean? Had she intended to add more?

Eileen closed the album and put it back in the drawer. She thought about the big, quiet man with the strange, restrained quality, the slow, easy smile, yet eyes that could be slate cold. Perhaps the answers she sought were in that little cottage by the lake. Certainly it had to hold some answers about Colin Riorden. A grim determination gathered inside her and she went downstairs, slipped from the house, pausing to see if Brannock were around to watch her, and made her way along the line of the garage and down to the road. Her eyes flicked for a moment to the little cemetery on the hill. The shadows were long now, deepening the small graveyard with the first fingers of coming night. She could just see the marble headstone at the top of the hill, the dark patch of violets in front of it, and the frown creased her brow again for a second. Then she hurried on, down the tree-covered stretch of road and onto the path which skirted the lough. She left the road then and began to crawl along the edge of the lough, keeping down below the top of the bank, and getting her feet wet as the waters lapped the shore. If he were in the cottage, she would wait. He was always prowling about as Molly had said.

He'd leave sooner or later. She had just reached the line of trees that grew along the bank, not far from where she had gone into the lough that first night, when she saw the door of the cottage open and Colin emerge. He surveyed the lough for a moment and then turned to walk across the road. She watched him as he went into the trees on the other side of the road where the land rose sharply. Peering over the top of the bank, she could see his figure moving upwards through the trees. The top of the hill would lead around to the far side of Drumroe, she knew, behind the little cemetery. From there one could watch the house unobserved. She waited, letting him move on higher, certain she had done the right thing coming to the cottage. Finally, when he was out of sight in the trees, she crawled forward, keeping behind the top of the bank. The sun had gone over the hills already and it would be dark soon. She didn't want to light any lights in the cottage and she hurried. She slipped on a muddy spot and fell to her knees in the water, swearing at herself. Then the cottage door was in front of her and she went in.

A small fire glowed in the little fireplace, and she was glad for the light it gave. Her eyes swept across the bed where she had wakened, naked, feeling so safe and secure and cozy. There was none of that feeling in her now as she began to scour the small room. The shelf of books were of no interest to her. Yet she quickly looked them over, opening each one and shaking it out. They seemed very new and hardly used. One, a *History of Celtic Civilization,* still had some of the pages uncut. She went on to the small desk, but it revealed nothing of interest. She moved quickly, but paused every few minutes to listen and to peer out the corner of the window. It was dark now, and she hoped she would hear him as he came back down the hill. It was very quiet here by the lough, deathly quiet, she thought grimly.

His clothes, mostly tweed jackets and trousers, hung in a small open closet space just off the tiny kitchen. She went through the pockets of each one, finding nothing and growing more frustrated and angry with every passing moment. He could come back at any moment and her visit had revealed absolutely nothing to her. She hadn't even found any notes or papers on the history of Ireland's leading families he said he was compiling and that was a bit odd, she thought. The cottage was mostly in darkness now, only the soft glow of the little fire casting a small circle of light directly in front of it. Groping along the tiny kitchen which had a small hot plate and a cupboard, her foot kicked something and she bent down to feel the smooth sides of an attaché case stuck almost behind the sink alongside the hot plate. She pulled it out and into the main room, kneeling down before the fire with it. Outside, she heard a sound and her heart froze. She listened and then heard it again, the wind rustling the leaves of the trees. She snapped open the attaché case. A little pad of yellow paper and a separate sheet of white paper were its sole contents. She took out the sheet and saw a list of names neatly typed on it. She felt her heart grow tighter as she read down the list. Each name had a small notation next to it.

Clarence Donegan: Found dead, apparent hit-run victim; Milford; 1958

Howell Donegan: Killed in fall from Routemaster bus, apparently drunk; London 1959

Albert MacAloor: Killed when car was hit by driverless truck; Castledera, 1960

William Donegan: Killed in robbery, criminal not apprehended; Belfast 1960

Terence Mulcane: Killed in boating accident; Donegal 1963

Cyril Donegan: Killed in fall from Belfast-Dublin Express; 1964

Thomas MacAloor: Died, Home for the Aged, overdose of sleeping pills, conclusion: suicide, 1961

Timothy Mulcane: Killed in hunting accident; Sligo, 1962

Michael Donegan: Suicide in apartment; London, 1965

Kenneth MacAloor: Jumped or fell from top floor of Home for the Aged; Dublin, 1966
Thomas Donegan: Drowning, fell from channel steamer, 1967
Joseph Mulcane: Confined to wheelchair, killed when wheelchair rolled off cliffs at Crohy Head, 1968
Terence Donegan: Killed in fall from building; London, 1970

Kenneth Donegan, Lord of Drumroe and Lady Donegan, died natural deaths in 1927 and 1933, respectively.

 Eileen felt her hand shaking, and the list of names she held danced as she stared at them. Some of them she knew, some she recognized at once, others she didn't know at all. But it was obvious that they were all members of the Donegan family, directly related or cousins and nephews. But what was Colin Riorden doing with this gruesome list? It recorded how each of them had met death over the past decade or so. They would all have been on in years with Terence Donegan, Aunt Agnes's youngest brother, probably sixty himself. But what did the list mean? Was it merely part of the history of the House of Drumroe he was compiling? Was it a chart showing that the Donegans were cursed with violence for all their peacemaking? If so, then perhaps Colin was indeed what he had said, an historian and nothing more. The thought made her feel better. Yet somehow, as she gazed down at the list, she knew there was more behind this morbid collection of recorded deaths. Outside, she heard the sound of a body moving through brush and trees, and her heart leaped in fright. Folding the list, she pushed it down into her rayon jersey and shoved the attaché case back behind the little sink. Through a corner of the window she saw the dark shape of his figure starting to cross the road. She went out the door headfirst, rolling down the side of the bank into a cluster of tall marsh grass. She lay there, on her stomach in the wetness, hidden in the tall grass and the dark. Her head turned on one side, she could see up the three feet of the bank to the top edge, and she saw Colin pause at the door that stood ajar. He came to the edge of the bank and his eyes probed across the lough, then back to the road. She couldn't see his eyes that well, but she knew they'd be hard as quartz and she lay very still. Finally he went back inside. She waited there till she saw the glow of the fire being stirred, and then she crept along the bank, half in the water and half out of it, holding her breath as she passed the cottage. When she reached the line of trees beyond she climbed up and onto the road and hurried toward Drumroe.

The dark towering house enveloped her as she flung the door open and hurried inside, an embrace not of warmth and security but of dark fear. Brannock was coming out of the kitchen as she ran up the stairs, and she caught the flash of white bandage on his hand, a grim reminder of the evil that seemed to surround her on all sides. Not that she needed reminding. She got out of the wet, mud-stained clothes at once, putting the list of names on her bed and donning a fresh dark green linen skirt and a lightweight maroon sweater. She went down and called Rory but there was no answer, and she returned to her room, putting the bolt on the door. Molly had asked her about dinner, but she had refused. Her stomach was tied up in knots. She opened the list and read it again, trying to make it mean something more than what it said. But the key, if there indeed were another meaning to it, eluded her. Yet there was another meaning, she was certain of it. She read down the list again. Thirteen names. Thirteen deaths neatly listed. Historical notations only? She wanted to hope so and yet she could not.

Tired, physically and mentally, she turned out the light, undressed, and went to the tall windows. The night mists were heavy, a swirling gray pink blanket on the ground. But there was something else, a figure at the far corner of the lawn, hurrying away, appearing and disappearing in the mists. She caught a last glimpse of long hair streaming out behind it and heard her own gasp of shock. Colin had climbed into the hills to circle around and spy on the house, and now the girl running from the scene. She wished Rory had come back earlier. She had the feeling of death all around her, of evil closing in to suffocate her. And as yet it all meant nothing, without reason or motive or plain sanity. If Aunt Agnes had been murdered, why? Why did the killer stalk a girl just here from a land three thousand miles away? But then, she reminded herself, madmen didn't need reasons, certainly not rational ones. The mad made madness its own motive, and perhaps the answer was as simple as that. But what madman? Certainly the old mullagh man was mad and perhaps his followers equally so. And Brannock's deep, haunted eyes certainly could hold the spark of madness. She had seen a kind of madness in the faces of those in the village square, a hate and anger that makes sane men mad. And Colin—did his changeable eyes that could go from cool amusement to warmth to gray slate hardness cloak a madness?

She lay down on the bed, drawing the sheet up to cover herself. Motive, that was the one possible road to finding the killer, she told herself. Even the mad had some kind of motive. The little list of names lay on the table beside her. It had to be a vital piece in this jigsaw puzzle of impending death. She stared at it, trying to make it reveal its meaning until she lay back again exhausted, and finally closed her eyes in restless sleep. Outside, the silver sheen of the moon reached over the ridge, and then the milk white edge of the void sphere began to rise. It grew larger as it rose, until it was round and full and glared down on the swirling mists of the ground below. High over the ridge it rose, sending its blue white light into the room where the girl slept, her flame-hair glowing on the pillow. She half-turned as the moonlight crept over her, and her red, full lips moved as she cried out softly. She spoke names that rose from the past, Emmet, Synge, Kevin Barry, Yeats, a liturgy born on the moonlight. Her voice grew stronger and she called out in her sleep. "Hush you look and hush you listen...like the banshees mournful tune...by the rising of the moon."

They had come, those names and many many more, on the rising of the moon when issues were joined and men marched to their moment of truth. They had come with flashing pikes to face death. The girl's head tossed from side to side, spilling her dark copper hair in wild profusion. And as the rising of the moon had called to many others, it spoke to her now, as she had predicted it would. Suddenly the girl sat upright, flinging the sheet from her body, her eyes wide, staring into the moonlit room.

"She's buried!" Eileen gasped out in the dark of the room. "In the little cemetery. She's buried in front of her headstone!"

Eileen leaped from the bed, threw the shirtwaist dress over her head, and grabbed a light-weight sweater. Aunt Agnes lay in the cemetery, buried by the killer, and Eileen knew why she suddenly was certain. But she had to see again, to prove the truth of her vision to herself. She unbolted the lock and flew down the darkened steps. Rushing out into the night, she was at once entangled in the wispy entrails of the mist. She ran to the garage and rummaged through the dashboard of the Jaguar, first, then the little Austin. In the latter she found a flashlight, small but strong enough to pierce the mist at close range. She ran out, between the house and the garage and up through the garden, feeling the slope of the hill beneath her feet.

But the trailing mists led her off to the right, and suddenly she realized she had reached the top of the hill and was not at the graveyard. She turned and moved forward slowly, feeling her way along the top line of the small hill with her steps. A swirl of mist tore aside for a moment and she glimpsed the headstones. But there was something else there, a figure in a raincoat. The mist closed in again and Eileen stood still for a long moment, instinctively crouching down. The rising of the moon would bring her answers, she knew, and perhaps more than she had realized. Above the swirling mists the silvery glow lighted the sky and the girl moved onward, inching her way, knowing that she could no more turn away and run than she could disregard the premonitions that came to seize her.

The mist shredded again for a moment and Eileen pressed her hand hard against her lips to stifle a gasp. The ground in front of the headstone had been shoveled away, and now a small mound of dirt rose there. The figure, with his back to her, rested the shovel on the mound. The mists came together again and Eileen crept forward, using the vaporous cover. Her hand gripping the flashlight was wet with perspiration and she switched hands while wiping her palm dry. Now, through the mists, the figure drifted into view like a partially developed photograph. Was it Brannock? She swallowed with difficulty. Or was it someone from the village, a total stranger, a madman? Or was it Colin? She couldn't tell size in the drifting mists that made the figure an ethereal thing. It might even be the old mullagh man, she reminded herself, though she doubted he owned a raincoat. She stepped forward, closer, close enough now. The figure took on more substance as the mists swirled away a little. Eileen drew her breath in sharply and switched on the flashlight. The figure spun around, the shovel still in hand, and she saw Colin Riorden's strong face peering at her, squinting as the light struck his eyes.

She heard the terrible sadness in her voice as she spoke. "So it was you," she gasped. She dropped the flashlight's beam to the mound of earth, not wanting to see into the hole he had dug. "Aunt Agnes," she said simply, knowing she was right.

"Yes," she heard Colin Riorden say. "She was there all the while."

Eileen lifted the flashlight into his face again. *"Murderer!"* she hissed, and now she suddenly realized what the list of names on the slip of paper had meant. "Aunt Agnes was the last of them," she said. "The last of the Donegans of Drumroe, except for me. That's why you tried to kill me, too. Did you kill all the others?"

"No, Eileen, listen to me," he said. "You don't understand." She saw him step forward toward her, his hands reach out for her, the hands that had just held the shovel, the hands of a murderer. She should have been terrified, but the terrible, all-consuming rage that swept through her flung everything else aside. She reached out with one hand, clawing at his face, and he pulled back in pain as she raked his temple, just missing his eyes.

"Damn you," he swore. He came in fast, head down, his long arms getting around her waist as she tried to claw at him again but only felt the top of his scalp. Then she brought the flashlight down, fury and desperation lending her strength she didn't really possess. She felt it hit, felt it shatter and go out. Colin Riorden's arms dropped their grip on her, and he pitched to the ground at her feet. He started to rise, groggy, shaking his head. She raised the flashlight to bring the battered remains of it down again when there was movement from out of the mists. A foot kicked out, catching Colin in the temple and sending him rolling onto his back unconscious. She looked up and saw Rory there, his eyes burning, hard, looking from her to the prone figure on the ground and sweeping past the unearthed ground.

"Oh, Rory, Rory!" she gasped, falling against his chest. "How did you know I was up here?"

"I got back late and I was worried about you," he said. "I drove out and got a glimpse of you heading up behind the house. I followed as best I could in the fog."

"Thank God for that," she gasped, trembling against him. The mists were lifting, a night wind suddenly coming up to blow them away like so many trailing gray bits of fabric. She looked down at Colin Riorden's unconscious form, and it was still hard for her to believe the strong, reassuring face was the face of a murderer. But there was only reality now, and she looked up at Rory. He was frowning as he looked at Colin.

"He was the one, Rory," she said. "He killed Aunt Agnes and tried to kill me. He had a whole list of names, all Donegans and relatives of the Donegans of Drumroe."

"Did he now?" Rory commented, a small smile edging his lips. Eileen found herself frowning at the smile, but people did strange things at times of stress and strain. Rory took her hand and started to pull her along the top of the hill, over to the other side of it. The trees were boldly outlined in the moonlight now, the mists completely evaporated.

"Where are you taking me?" Eileen asked.

"Someplace where you'll be safe," Rory said. "He'll be out for a spell, but it may take a while to get the guards here at this time of night. He could come to, get away, and go after you again."

"Let's go back to the house and take the car," Eileen said. "I can hide at your place."

"No, it's too likely a place. He'd look for you there, if he didn't find you anywhere else," Rory said. "You'll be safe where I'm taking you."

He was moving fast, pulling her along and she sensed the excitement in him. She wished she could feel as flushed with victory, but all she felt was empty, hollow, with a lot of questions still unanswered. He was leading her up a steep trail that turned into deep woods, pulling her along firmly.

"I've been suspicious of him ever since he moved into that cottage," he said. "Historian," he snorted. "It was his cover. So he had the list, did he?"

Eileen nodded as he glanced at her, the small smile edging his lips again. "All thirteen of them and he had them all on the list," he repeated, musing aloud.

Eileen felt her heart stop and go silent for a long moment. A small explosion went off inside her and mushroomed with terrifying speed. She stood still, pulling her hand free.

"I didn't tell you there were thirteen names on that list, Rory," she said quietly. He looked down at her, grinned, the lock of sandy hair falling boyishly over his forehead.

Eileen suddenly realized his knee seemed to be very much back in place. In fact, he had kicked hard with it at Colin's temple.

"How did you know there were thirteen names on that list, Rory?" she asked, her face frozen.

"I knew because I made that list possible," he grinned at her. Eileen felt herself quivering, icy with terror.

"You... you're in this together? You and Riorden?"

"You could say that," he said and she saw his eyes glitter with a wild, maniacal triumph. "Only I won. It was a sort of a race, I guess. But I saw to it that the great Lady Donegan will be the fourteenth name on that list."

"You killed Aunt Agnes?" Eileen gasped, recoiling in shocked horror. His tight smile gave his answer.

"You were an unexpected problem," he said. "You and your damned luck and your premonitions."

Everything was falling into place, the unanswered questions being answered. Most of them, at least.

"The tree beside the lough," she said, her voice straining to even form the sentence. "It was you then." She went on, not waiting for his answer, knowing it now. "Of course, you knew I was coming," she said. "You'd tried to keep me from coming, but then insisted on it when Aunt Agnes was adamant."

"You could have gone back," he said, a sudden note of petulant anger in his voice. "I told you to leave, but you wouldn't listen."

"At the shantully, you severed the rope of the footbridge when you came back with the wine," she said, seeing it all so cleverly now. "And then you faked that trick knee. You were very clever. You didn't even ask me to go for the bandage. You just waited, knowing I would volunteer, knowing I'd insist. If your plan didn't work out, and it didn't, I couldn't suspect you at all."

His smile widened into a grin of deadliness. She was going to ask why Colin had pulled her to safety if they were in this together, but he suddenly sprang at her, his hand seizing her by the throat, the same hand that had seized her that afternoon while she watched the old mullagh man. Glancing down, she saw the ugly tear of her teeth marks on his skin. He had been the one following her, not Colin. Yet he had implied it was Colin. It had been a kind of race, he had said. A race between two madmen? She felt herself spun around, his arms pulling her wrist up tight behind her, and she gasped in pain.

"Keep walking," he said. "This isn't the place I have picked out for you. You are going to be number fifteen on that list."

She spoke to him, in between the shooting pains as he kept her wrist twisted behind her. She had to know why. It still made no sense. She had to have an answer, even if it were only to know that he was insane.

"Why, Rory, why?" she gasped. He halted, pulled her arm up tighter behind her and she screamed in pain. She heard his laugh and glanced back, twisting her head to do so. His handsome, boyish face was contorted with hate, a frightening caricature of itself.

"Old debts and old accounts paid in full," he snarled at her. "And an evil wiped out, the evil that's passed down in the Donegans of Drumroe from the time of the witch. It's in you, too, I found that out quickly enough."

"You're mad, Rory," she said. "You're sick. There's no evil passed down." She looked at him, still not knowing the answer, but seeing only that she would be killed. Death and fiery hate filled his eyes. Then she would be killed fighting, at least, the girl vowed in her own, grim anger. She raised her foot and brought it down hard on his, scraping it along the ankle and onto the instep. His grip relaxed for a moment as he reacted in pain, and she tore away, clawing out at him as she did, raking his cheek with her nails. He lunged for her again, but she was running through the trees, using the trunks to swing herself forward from one to the other in a cross pattern. He lunged for her, cursing, his hands slipping from hers as she swung herself around the trees. She stumbled, fell to one knee and he was on her at once, his hands closing around her copper hair and yanking her head back. But her own hand had closed around a rock as she fell. Screaming in pain as he pulled her back by the hair, she flung the rock into his face, smashing it against his nose. Once more he let go and cursed in pain. His hand flew to his face, and she saw the blood gush out from between his fingers.

She ran, straight this time, racing down the way he had brought her. But he was coming after her again, running faster than she could, a dark shape, the figure of death chasing her down. She dodged to the right, then the left as he almost caught up to her. She glanced around in desperation, looking for something, some weapon, a piece of wood, another stone. But there was nothing. Her breath was dry, rasping, and only terror kept her legs going. There was a small clearing ahead, and she raced for it. His arm grabbed hers, pulling her back. She ducked his other arm as he tried to bring it around her throat, and clawed out at his face again, blood streaming down his jaws. But he blocked her hands, his fist coming up in a short arc. She took the blow on the side of her head as she twisted away, but it was enough to send her sprawling out beyond the edge of the trees and into the cleared area. Her head was swimming and she was only dimly aware of his hands tightening around her throat. But she heard the shot ring out, splitting the night with its sharp crack. The fingers around her throat loosened and she heard his body fall beside her, shudder, and lie still.

She shook her head and her vision returned. Rory lay on his side, crumpled, and she was being pulled to her feet. She saw Colin Riorden standing there, the gun in his hand. He reached out for her and she shrank away.

"No," she gasped. "You're both involved in this. You're in it together, somehow. You're madmen, both of you."

But she couldn't run any more. She had cheated death only to have it stare her in the face again.

"You're half right," he said. "I'm involved, but not the way you think. Why do you think I came after you just now? Molly brought me around. She'd seen you run off in the mist from her window. When you didn't come back, she went out looking for you and found me. Why didn't I just take off and run then?"

"I don't know," Eileen almost shouted in despair. "I don't know anything and I don't understand any of it."

"But you don't trust me," he said.

"No, I don't trust you," she replied. "I can't."

He waved the gun at her. "Walk," he said. "Over the top of the hill and to the house. Rory Malachy's dead. There's nothing left to do here now."

"Rory Muldoon," she corrected, frowning.

"Malachy," he said. "Walk."

She turned and walked quickly, trying to assemble her thoughts, trying to figure out what the big man meant by calling Rory by the name Malachy. The name meant something, but she couldn't make it fit. Her mind was a frightened jumble, too terrorized to think. As she crossed the top of the ridge the house loomed up, stark in the moonlight, like some prehistoric monument to another age. Perhaps that was what it really was, she reflected.

Colin Riorden was behind her, holding the gun. They entered the house. He waved her into the library and handed her the phone.

"Is there anyone getting your mail back in the States?" he asked.

She nodded. "Sarah and Sam Grossman, my neighbors," she answered.

"Call them," he said. "Now. It'll be morning there. There's a letter there for you from Scotland Yard."

She was frowning incredulously. "How do you know that?" she asked.

"My superior sent it, Inspector Rodgers. Dial the overseas operator. You shouldn't have trouble getting through at this hour."

She dialed, looking at Colin Riorden as she did. She gave the operator Sarah and Sam's number and waited. It took only a few minutes, and then she heard Sarah's voice, bursting into excitement when she realized it was Eileen calling.

"I can't really talk now, Sarah," Eileen said. "But I need some information, important information. Is there a letter there for me from Scotland Yard?"

"Yes, it came just after you'd left," she heard Sarah say. "Here, I've got it in my hand. Shall I open it?"

"Yes, please," Eileen said, her eyes on Colin as she listened.

"Dear Miss Donegan," she heard Sarah's voice come back on the wire. "We have learned that your aunt, Lady Donegan, may write you and ask you to come over to Drumroe. Please contact me at the number on this letterhead if she does. Please call collect. Under no circumstances come to Drumroe until you have contacted me. We have reason to believe it could place your life in jeopardy. Respectfully, Inspector Harry Rodgers."

"Thanks, Sarah," Eileen said softly. "I'll call you again later. Say hello to Sam."

She hung up and her knees were suddenly very weak. She sank down into the chair beside the small telephone table. Colin put the gun into his pocket, and she saw the deep sigh that drained out of him. He sank down on the couch, looking very tired. She found enough strength to move over to him and sit beside him.

"You are from Scotland Yard," she said. "I'm sorry, Colin. If only I'd known."

"You couldn't have," he said, managing a smile.

"That's why you looked at me with such shocked surprise that morning at the lough," she said, another of the pieces falling into place.

"Yes, I thought you were safe in the States, and there you were in front of me," he said. "But you were of help, though you didn't know it. When you told me of your very strange accident,

I knew I hadn't wasted the months I'd spent posing as an historian. The man we were after was indeed here, someplace. I'm only sorry I couldn't have found him before he struck once again. He was hurried into that when he learned your aunt had finally sent for you, and your cable came giving your arrival date."

"I caused her death, then," Eileen said.

"No, I'm afraid he'd have struck anyway," Colin said. "Your arrival only hurried him a little."

"But why, Colin? I still don't understand. What did the list mean?"

"So you have the list?" he said, his eyebrows lifting. "You were the one in the cottage? I knew someone had been there when the door was ajar, and I found the list was missing rightaway. But I thought the killer had gotten onto me somehow."

"No, I took it," she admitted, feeling ashamed. His slow smile made her feel better. There was even a tinge of reluctant admiration in it.

"Who was Rory Muldoon or Malachy?" she asked.

"Terence Malachy's son," Colin answered. "Terence Malachy, the man who led the Fifth Brigade which was almost wiped out by the English that night I told you about."

Eileen nodded. "When they couldn't cut through Drumroe land and escape," she said.

"Exactly," he said. "Everyone thought it was a closed chapter, tragic but closed. Most people thought Terence Malachy dead. We certainly never even heard of him at the Yard until we began digging back into things. How we started to dig back was the result of a purely routine review of certain accidents. Well, perhaps not purely routine. When Terence Donegan was killed in that fall in London some months ago, we weren't satisfied it was an accident. We began checking into his background and found the listing of the deaths of Thomas and Joseph Donegan. Then we got into the deaths of his cousin, Joseph Mulcane. Suddenly the thing began to build itself into a very intriguing pattern. We found that a

Donegan or a close relative had been killed every year since 1958; some of those deaths were unsatisfactorily explained at the time, but lack of evidence had closed the cases. We traced further and found out that each of the dead men had been part of the House of Drumroe, part of those keeping the Drumroe land neutral on the night of that battle with the English.

"I'm attached to the Dublin branch of the yard, and I got into most of that spade work. Our London men discovered the fact that Terence Malachy hadn't died, but had been a fence for stolen goods in the dock section, as I told you. But we also found that he'd sired a son by a local prostitute. The son had been involved in scrapes with the police and had been confined to a home for mentally disturbed children for a spell. But he was released finally and returned to his father. We had found out a lot, but we were still without actual evidence. However, we were convinced that every one of those thirteen men had been murdered, one a year, each one cleverly and carefully set up. Thomas MacAloor, for instance, who died of an overdose of sleeping pills in a home for the aged. On checking back we found that the attendant who had taken care of him, a young man, had quit his job at the hospital soon after and disappeared. Thomas Donegan, who drowned when he fell from a channel steamer during a crossing, had come aboard with a young man, a traveling companion who just vanished after the accident. Then we learned that on Terence Malachy's death in 1957 his son had made a strange, wild speech of revenge during the services and then vanished completely."

"He had made it his mission to avenge his father," Eileen commented softly. "Twisted hatred, warped, insane." Instilled in him or in some way inherited, she asked herself silently and didn't pursue the thought, shuddering with it.

"That's clear now," Colin said. "We had a picture in our minds when we got into this thing. We had discovered a pattern of murders cleverly disguised as accidents. We had the motive, vengeance. We even had the probable killer, only he was unknown to any of us, a shadowy figure. We couldn't even come up with a description of him. But we had one more thing, the calculated guess that he would strike again at the last living member of the Donegans of Drumroe, your aunt. We hoped to get him in time. I came here posing as an historian, checking out every newcomer in the area and watching your aunt's movements. We had men watching every major station and crossroad in and out of the area around Cladvale. I failed in spite of it all. Dammit, I'd give anything to have the chance to do it over."

Eileen's hand reached out to touch his face. "Don't blame yourself, Colin," she said. "Some things no one can prevent. Fate holds the reins on them. Maybe if I hadn't come, if there'd been more time, you could have."

"Your coming triggered him into action, all right," Colin said. "I'd be pretty certain he didn't even know you existed until your aunt told him she was going to send for you to sign the papers as the last direct heir to Drumroe. When you cabled you were arriving, he had to act and act quickly. Then, of course, he had to kill you because you were in line to keep the House of Drumroe alive."

"When he failed that first time at the lough, he tried to get me to go home," Eileen recalled aloud. "When he realized I wouldn't, I guess he decided I had to be killed once and for all."

"You were also determined to keep probing into your aunt's disappearance," Colin said. "But we knew that if you came here you'd be in danger, just as we were sure your aunt was in danger. When I learned from her that she'd sent for you, I had my boss send that letter that just missed you."

"I suspected Brannock," Eileen said. "Or even that crazy old mullagh man. Why was Brannock so hostile to me?"

"I was onto him long ago," Colin said. "He was running guns and arms to the rebels in Ulster, using the basement of the house as a storeroom. He didn't have trouble keeping it from your aunt. She wasn't given to poking around down there any longer. But he was afraid you'd come onto his sideline, so he wasn't happy to see you appear, either. The old mullagh man is more weird than harmful, though you were in danger that time you stumbled on their ceremony."

"But the girl with the long black hair," Eileen asked. "I saw her running away earlier tonight."

"Yes, I saw her hiding in the trees when I looked over the grounds," he said.

"But why was she there?" Eileen probed.

"Most likely the old man sent her to see if you were at the house or not," Colin said. "I'd guess they had one of their druidic ceremonies planned for tonight and wanted to find out if you were about spying."

"How would I know whether they'd planned a ceremony?" Eileen asked, indignant at the thought.

"Witches have all kinds of ways of knowing things," Colin answered and she shot a quick, glaring glance at him. His face was expressionless, but his eyes were laughing and she felt herself smile.

"I guess I fail the witch test," she said. "I should have known a lot more than I did if I were any good as a witch."

"I'd agree there," he said, and she saw his eyes harden. "And I'm not much better as a detective," he said. "I didn't suspect him at all. He was already set up here as your aunt's solicitor when I arrived, of course."

"When Aunt Agnes's lifelong lawyer died, Rory apparently saw his opportunity and came here at once, a briefcase full of false credentials no doubt. He sold her a bill of goods and convincingly, that's obvious. But what happens now with Brannock and the old man?"

"I'll have my people round them both up, and the proper charges will be brought against them," Colin said. Eileen saw the depth of feeling in the big, quiet man's eyes, a disconsolate unhappiness, and she pressed her hand over his. "You did your best, Colin," she said. "He had to have been clever, terribly clever, to have committed all the other murders without being detected. But then the mad can be terribly clever."

She pressed her hand on his, looking into the gray blue eyes that were now very sad and very tired.

"I must say you had me fooled," she said. "When I told you of my premonition about Aunt Agnes being dead, I was convinced you didn't believe me."

"I didn't," he said. "Your aunt knew who I was. I'd told her the day she informed me she'd written you to come." Eileen saw the little slip of paper with Colin's name in the album. So that's what the three exclamation points meant, a personal reminder for herself.

"I meant what I said to you about murder not being that easy to pull off," Colin said. "Certainly not with me watching everything, and we had men watching every junction out of the area. If he'd killed her and tried to drive her out of the area, we'd have caught him. Frankly, I thought, or maybe I just hoped, your aunt had fled into hiding, that she'd been suddenly frightened, perhaps came onto something and been unable to reach me and had fled. But then, when you kept saying that something about the plot by her headstone bothered you, I decided to take a gamble on that undefined uneasiness of yours. What made you suddenly rush up there tonight?"

"The bed of violets," she answered. "They were what bothered me, but I couldn't put it together. Then I woke up tonight and I had the answer. Half the bed of violets, those in the foreground, were turned to the sun, the way all wild flowers grow. But the others in the rear half of the square were turned away, facing in the wrong direction. They were wild flowers. They wouldn't, they couldn't have grown that way. The land had been carefully cut out and dug up so as not to damage the square bed of flowers. But those in the back section had been put back facing the wrong way."

Colin's face was grim. "Yes," he said. "He must have suspected we were on the watch. Burying her in the little cemetery was convenient and clever. I wouldn't have looked if it hadn't been for you being bothered. You know, you'd do pretty well in Scotland Yard."

He was smiling at her, the slow, warm, reassuring smile. He leaned forward. "There's no sense posing as a prim and proper historian anymore," he said, kissing her. His arms encircled her, and she felt safe and warm and happy, a bittersweet kind of happiness, but happy nonetheless.

"You'll not stay here at Drumroe, will you?" he asked, pulling back. She shook her head no.

"I've a good bit of vacation coming," he said. "I'm thinking of visiting the States."

"I'd like that," she said. "I'd like that very much."

"There are some people there I'd like to get to know better," he said, his eyes twinkling, all the hardness gone from them. "I might even get married while I'm there."

She met his steady gaze levelly. "I'll be sure to be at the wedding," she said. She kissed him hard, hungrily, and then settled her head against his chest. She had come back here to find new meaning to her life, to find her roots, and she had indeed found them. She had learned to be afraid of the outside things and not herself. Her clairvoyance and premonitions could no longer frighten her. She had learned not to run from them, that they didn't possess her any more than her hair or her eyes or her desire for love possessed her. The other voices, the visions, and the insights were a part of her to live with, to accept, and perhaps, to more fully understand. Resting in Colin's arms, she knew she had found herself and so this time she could find happiness. There'd be no desperate fleeing from herself this time, no looking away from truth. Instead of searching, there'd be finding, instead of brass, there'd be gold.

And of this lovely land, clinging to so many things, place of so many contrasts, she recalled how William Butler Yeats had once written of that Easter in 1916:

All changed, changed utterly:
A terrible beauty is born.

Perhaps it would be that way once again, a terrible beauty born from the anguish and agony. It was going to be that way for her, she knew. She lifted her face to Colin and felt the stirring touch of his lips again.

"Do you travel a lot in your work, Colin?" she asked.

"A good deal," he said. "It'd be helpful to have someone along a lot of the time, especially someone well taken to predicting things." His slow smile curled her up in his arms again and she wondered if Molly might like to cook for a young married couple who traveled a good deal.

GLOSSARY

BULLANS: stones with bowl-shaped hollows; thought to be relics of pagan rites.

CAHIR: stone fort

COLCANNON: green cabbage, mashed potatoes, scallions, and meat

CROMLECHS: often called Druids' Altars; giant slabs of stone standing on end and covered by a horizontal capstone; relics of ancient druidic ceremonies of pre-Christian Ireland

CROPPIES: Irish rebels of the 1798 uprising named "croppies" by the English because of short-cropped hair

DRUM: ridge

GAL: stranger

GALLANS: tall and massive stones standing on end, often in groups, believed to be ancient pagan idols or worshipping stones

LOUGH: lake

MULLAGH: summit

PRATIES: potatoes

RASHERS: bacon

RATH: ancient Bronze Age earthen forts

ROE: red

SHAN: old

SOUTERRAINS: uncemented stone chambers and connecting passages dating to pagan era, used as places of refuge

TULLY: hillock

TUMULI: earthen burial mounds of the pre-Christian era, often decorated with carvings

IRISH GREEN OR ERIN SAUCE

12-ounce chopped spinach (fresh or frozen)
2 tablespoons butter (or margarine)
2 tablespoons flour
1/2 teaspoon salt
2 dashes pepper (black pepper preferred)
1 egg yolk
1-1/4 cup light cream
1/4 cup milk
1-1/2 tablespoons lemon juice

Cook spinach well. While spinach cooks, melt butter in saucepan and remove from heat. Stir in flour, salt, and pepper preferably with a wooden spoon. When smooth, stir in the cream.

Over medium heat, bring to boil and stir constantly. Reduce heat and simmer until sauce is thickened (about 3 - 4 minutes). Stir in spinach and some of the cooking liquid. Do not thin sauce too much.

Using fork, beat egg yolk slightly in the milk.

Stir a small amount of the hot sauce into yolk-milk mixture until well-mixed.

Pour this back into saucepan, cook over a low heat while stirring constantly until sauce is thoroughly heated.

Stir in lemon juice until completely blended. Do not allow sauce to darken by too much heat. Serve when thoroughly heated.